D1107700

Erickson, John R., 1943-
The incredible ice event /
2022.
~~30000000000008~~
cu   12/06/22

The Incredible Ice Event

John R. Erickson

Illustrations by Nicolette G. Earley
in the style of Gerald L. Holmes

Maverick Books, Inc.

MAVERICK BOOKS, INC.
Published by Maverick Books, Inc.
P.O. Box 549, Perryton, TX 79070
Phone: 806.435.7611
www.hankthecowdog.com

First published in the United States of America by Maverick Books, Inc. 2022.

1 3 5 7 9 10 8 6 4 2

Copyright © John R. Erickson, 2022

All rights reserved

LIBRARY OF CONGRESS CONTROL NUMBER: 2022939092

978-1-59188-178-0 (paperback); 978-1-59188-278-7 (hardcover)

Hank the Cowdog® is a registered trademark of John R. Erickson.

Printed in the United States of America

Except in the United States of America, this book is sold subject
to the condition that it shall not, by way of trade or otherwise, be lent,
re-sold, hired out, or otherwise circulated without the publisher's
prior consent in any form of binding or cover other than that in which
it is published and without a similar condition including this
condition being imposed on the subsequent purchaser.

I dedicate this book to the memory of Baxter Black, an incredible talent and a dear friend.

CONTENTS

CHAPTER ONE

Drover Ate
A Tick

I t's me again, Hank the Cowdog. The mystery began in February, as I recall. Yes, it was February and here's how I know. Pay attention.

In Texas, February is the only month that begins with an **F** and ends in a **Y**, with six letters in between. Hencely, the mystery couldn't possibly have begun in March, Tuesday, or Tennessee. Here, check this out:

- March begins with an **M** and ends with an **H**, so we can throw it out right away.
- Tuesday has seven letters and it's not even a month, so it's out too.
- Tennessee: Every town in Texas has a February but there are no Texas towns in Tennessee, so Tennessee has no chance.

1

Pretty impressive, huh? You bet. How many dogs could figure this stuff out? Not many. Most of your ordinary mutts don't know the difference between a calendar and a cauliflower, but I do. A calendar is what you keep on the wall beside the telephone and a cauliflower is...I don't know, some kind of posey. A flower.

The point is, we didn't know if Tennessee had February that year but Texas sure did and it was fixing to turn cold, the kind of scary cold we'd never seen before. We didn't know it was coming and you're not supposed to know either, so just forget I said anything about it.

As far as we're concerned, it was an ordinary February. We'd had a little snow and some cold temperatures but nothing scary.

The Security Division had moved most of our winter operations down to Slim Chance's shack, two miles east of ranch headquarters, because... well, he lets us sleep inside the house and that's very important in Security Work. Our troops were well-rested and we had settled into the normal routine of feeding cattle six days a week.

Some days, Slim had to chop ice on the stock tanks but it hadn't been bad. See, a hard freeze puts a layer of ice on the surface and Slim breaks it up with a chopping ax, so the cattle can drink.

They need water, you know, and in February we expect to chop some ice.

So, yes, it was a Wednesday and we were in the midst of our daily feed run. We were between pastures, chugging down the Wolf Creek road at Slim's usual speed of about twenty miles an hour. I was riding Shotgun, as always, and Drover sat in the middle of the seat.

It was kind of a slow time and he dozed off…and maybe I did too. Nothing serious, just a short nap.

All at once, the brakes screeched and I went flying into the dashboard. That woke me up and I shot a glare at Slim. See, when he gets bored and catches me napping, he slams on the brakes to wake me up. He thinks it's funny.

He wore a sly grin so I knew this was another of his stale jokes. "Wake up, pooch. You're working for the ranch today, so snap out of it."

Very funny.

"Would it help if I sang y'all a song?"

What? No, please, not another corny song.

"I've got the title but I'm still working on the words. I call it, 'When I Tried To Give My Dog a Job, He Couldn't Stay Awake.' What do you think?"

This was unbelievable—a grown man, a tax-paying citizen, who didn't have anything better to do than torment his dogs.

He whispered behind his hand. "I think my agent in Nashville will snap it up. I'll keep working on it."

His agent in Nashville. Oh brother. This was so...never mind.

Just then he noticed a pickup stopped in the middle of the road up ahead of us. The driver had his arm out the window, telling us to stop. Slim took a closer look. "Uh oh, that's Woodrow. What have I done this time?"

Woodrow, you might recall, was a grumpy old rancher who lived down the creek a couple of miles. He didn't seem very friendly to anyone, especially the cowboy-pauper who had slipped an engagement ring on his daughter's finger.

If Slim ever got around to marrying Miss Viola, Woodrow would be his daddy-in-law and neither one of them seemed thrilled about that.

Slim pulled up beside the pickup and there sat Woodrow, wearing a winter cap and insulated coveralls. He had bushy eyebrows and a mouth that looked like a piece of wet rope.

They nodded a greeting and Woodrow said, "I guess you've been watching the weather on TV."

"I don't own a TV and don't want one."

"Well, I'm not trying to sell you one, but a man needs to pay attention to the weather report.

4

Sometimes it's important. Do you own a radio?"

"Yes."

"Do you ever turn it on?"

"Sometimes, when I get to craving noise and bad news."

Woodrow gave his head a shake and stared straight ahead. "Everybody who lives out here gets odd, but you're leading the pack."

"If I was to turn on my radio, what would I learn?"

"It's fixing to turn cold."

"Woodrow, it always turns cold in February, and it don't matter whether I listen to the radio or not."

"This is a different deal, Arctic cold. Get prepared. Wrap your pipes and run a drip in the sink. Have some candles handy in case the power goes off. And turn on your radio."

That was it. He drove off.

Slim laughed out loud. "That old man didn't just flunk out of charm school, he got expelled. I can't believe Viola's a branch off his family tree. It's like a pretty flower growing on a cholla cactus." He turned his gaze on me. "Reckon we ought to turn on the radiator?"

Huh? Was he talking to me?

He reached out his hand and turned on the radio, which brought a blast of static. He shut it off and muttered, "Oh yeah, the antenna's busted. I didn't want to listen anyway."

He put the pickup in gear and we headed on down the road to the next pasture. I turned to Drover. "Did you hear any of that?"

"Oh, hi. Any of what?"

"The conversation between Woodrow and Slim."

"Who's Woodrow?"

I could feel my temperature rising. "The man in the other pickup, you weed."

"Oh, him. Well, let's see. I think he said...his ticks are cold.'"

"His ticks? You think he has ticks?"

"Yeah, I had one on my ear last summer, a big fat one."

"Never mind, I don't want to hear about your ticks."

"I scratched it off and ate it. Hee hee."

I stared at the runt. "You ate a tick? That's disgusting."

"It was better than you'd think. It made a nice crunch."

"Oh brother. Do you know what that tick had been eating?"

"Something red. Spaghetti?"

"No. *Your blood.*"

His silly grin vanished. "You're fooling."

6

"Drover, if it was on your ear, it was drinking your blood. That's what ticks do for a living. You ate your own blood."

"Oh my gosh. What if I turn into a vampire?"

"You'll grow long teeth and lose all your friends."

"Oh my gosh! Mom'll be so disappointed!"

"Of course. There isn't a mother in Texas who wants to hear that she raised a vampire."

"She was afraid I'd be a bum, but now...this!" It appeared that he would start bawling.

"Wait. Before you fall to pieces, let me check this out. Open your mouth and say 'ahhh.'" He opened wide and I peered inside. "Hmm. Your tongue's in the right place and I don't see any fangs. I think you might be all right."

"Han I hose eye outh?"

"What? Speak up."

"Han I hose eye outh?"

"Drover, I can't understand you when your mouth is hanging open. Close your mouth and try again."

He closed his mouth. "I said, can I close my mouth?"

"You've already closed it. How many times do you need to close one mouth?"

"I'm not feeling so good. I drank my own blood."

"Oh rubbish. That was six months ago. I did

7

a complete physical and there's nothing wrong with you."

"Yeah, but tick rhymes with sick." His head began moving up and down and he started making those sounds a dog makes when he's about to toss his cookies. "Ump, ump, ump."

Slim heard it too. "Hey, not in my pickup!"

He pulled off into the ditch, threw open the door, and tossed the little sickling outside. Slim and I

8

looked away while he did his business. A sick dog deserves some privacy, even if he's a hypocardiac.

I'm sorry to end the chapter with Drover barfing, but it's not my fault. I have to deal with Reality as it really is. You might want to turn the page and keep reading.

Arctic Has Nothing To Do With Ticks or Ducks

Does any of this make sense? Back in the summer, Drover ate a tick. He remembered it six months later and threw up, because tick rhymes with sick. What can you say?

Well, he wasn't kidding about being sick. He took care of the nasty business and we got back on the road. Slim was shaking his head and muttering under his breath. "I've got the two barfingest dogs in the whole Texas Panhandle. How could I be so lucky? The next one of y'all that throws up in my pickup..."

He didn't finish the sentence but we got the message. And let the record show that I had nothing to do with this fiasco. As for Slim's cruel remark that he owned "the two barfingest dogs" in the whole Panhandle...well, that hurt. It was pure slander and further proof that no dog can please these people.

When we barf, we get blamed. When we don't barf, we still get blamed. Phooey.

Drover seemed to be in a chirpy mood. "Boy, that helped. I feel better."

"Good. I'm glad you're feeling better, but I've got some bad news."

His grin faded. "Oh no. I'm still going to be a vampire?"

"Stop talking about vampires and ticks. While you were barfing your head off, I figured out what Woodrow said. He was talking about *ducks*, not ticks. He said, 'Our ducks are cold.' Ducks are not ticks."

"Gosh, you mean..."

"Yes. Viola must be raising ducks. You garbled the transfusion and got us into a loony conversation about a tick you ate six months ago."

"You said 'transfusion' but I think you meant 'translation.'"

"I don't care. Viola is raising ducks."

"Gosh. So...I got sick over a duck?"

"Yes, you got sick over a duck and you didn't even eat one. You wasted a good breakfast and made the entire Security Division look ridiculous.

For that, you get five Chicken Marks."

"If it was a duck, how come I get Chicken Marks?"

I stared into the emptiness of his eyes and felt a snarl twitching on my lips. "Because, Drover, the Security Division doesn't give Duck Marks for punishment. We give Chicken Marks."

"Oh, I get it, 'cause they're both birds?"

"Exactly my point. A chicken will never be a duck and a duck will never be a chicken, but they both will be birds forever."

"I'll be derned. Birds forever. You know, I feel a lot better."

"Good. We'll add five more Chicken Marks and see how you feel. This will go into my report and please don't speak to me again."

I turned my back on the little goose and didn't speak to him through the rest of the morning feed run. Wait, hold everything. Check this out:

- Goose
- Chicken
- Duck
- They all have wings and feathers.
- All three will be birds foreverly.

Was this some kind of clue that might propel the case to a higher level? No. Skip it.

The point is that I ignored him for the rest of

the morning. When he started moaning because he never gets to ride in the Shotgun Position, I didn't listen or answer. This gives you a glimpse into what I have to put up with in this job. He lures me into these...these crazy conversations that go into spirals, like dirty water spinning around a sink drain, and somehow...

Never mind. The point is that you can't find good help any more.

We spent the morning feeding cattle on the east side of the ranch, then drove back to headquarters to load up more feed for the cattle in the north pastures. It had turned into a beautiful winter day, the kind we don't expect in February. The sun was out, the sky was clear, and the wind was as soft as a feather.

Loper's parkup was picked in front of the machine shed...wait, hold everything. Loper's *pickup* was *parked* in front of the machine shed. You see what he does to me? Drover, that is. He gets me so messed up, I can hardly talk.

Loper's pickup was parked in front of the machine shed and that's where we went. He was holding a funnel in one hand and a plastic container in the other, pouring some kind of fluid into the fuel tank of his pickup.

Slim said, "What's that?"

"Diesel treatment."

"Treatment for what?"

"Have you been listening to the radio?"

Slim heaved a sigh. "No. The radio in my pickup don't work because a bale of hay slid off the load and busted the antenna, and the man I work for is too cheap to buy a new one."

Loper smirked. "Smart man. But I thought you wired a coat hanger to the stub."

"I did but it fell off."

"Poor workmanship. Don't you have a radio at the house?"

"I do but it don't work either, because I don't turn it on. How come everybody wants to know if I'm listening to the radio? Don't a man have a right to some peace and quiet?"

Loper removed the funnel and screwed the cap back on the fuel tank. "The radio station in Twitchell has a new feature. They call it the *weather report*. If you listen, you become less ignorant about what the weather's going to do. Some people would rather be informed than ignorant."

"Loper, I make my own weather report. I walk out on my porch and look at the thermometer. If it says hot, I don't wear a coat. If it says cold, I bundle up. If water's pouring off the roof, I know it's likely to rain. I don't need some disc jockey to tell me what I can see for myself."

Loper sighed and shook his head. "Boy, you've got a bad case of the iron-head. No wonder you're still a bachelor."

Slim hitched up his jeans. "By grabs, there's a woman down the creek who's wearing my engagement ring."

"She's a saint and was misinformed. If she ever gets to know you, she'll trade that ring for a pair of five-buckle overshoes."

Slim laughed. "Boy, you're on a snort today, and so was Woodrow. Y'all-two are so alike, it's scary."

"You saw Woodrow?"

"I did, yes. It was my bad luck to meet him in the middle of the county road this morning. He said the radio said it's fixing to turn cold. I explained that this is February and it's supposed to be cold, and I don't need a radio to figure it out."

Loper looked up at the sky. "Slim, they're not talking about a normal cold spell. They're talking about a polar vortex."

"Never heard of it."

"Well, that's the point. It's is a huge Arctic cold front that's going to put us in the deep freeze for a whole week."

"Huh. How cold are we talking about?"

"Eight inches of snow and wind chills of thirty

below."

Slim's eyebrows shot up. "Thirty below! Good honk, that don't sound good."

"In that kind of cold, everything quits working. Pipes freeze, diesel pickups don't start, power lines break, cattle suffer, and stock tanks freeze over. This one scares me."

Slim licked his lips. "Okay, now you're scaring me. What's the plan?"

"It's supposed to move in this afternoon, so we've got half a day to prepare. Sally May's going to town to stock up on groceries and buy more diesel treatment, extension cords, and heat tape. We need to plug in our diesels tonight. Leave a drip going on faucets and draw a bathtub full of water. We need to stock up on firewood and I hope the chainsaws work. We'd better carry an ax and a shovel in both pickups."

"There goes my afternoon nap."

"Sally May's got a pot of chicken soup on the stove. Let's grab a quick lunch and get to work. It's going to be a long afternoon."

They headed for the house, leaving me and Drover alone in front of the machine shed. I still wasn't speaking to the little wretch, or even looking at him, but he spoke first. "I just figured it out."

I swung my gaze around and forked him with

two piercing eyes. "What?"

"I just figured it out."

"If you figured something out, it's the biggest news of the year."

"Gosh, thanks."

"Get to the point and hurry up. What do you think you figured out?"

He beamed a silly grin. "See, you thought Woodrow said 'Our ducks are cold,' but he was talking about *Arc-tic cold*. I'll bet they don't have any ducks. Hee hee. You were wrong."

Huh? Wrong? That word came down on me like a hammer. I whirled away and began pacing, as I often do when my mind seems clouded by clouds. The little ninny had scored a point and it really hurt.

"All right, maybe I was misquoted. Arctic has nothing to do with ducks."

He was almost beside himself. "See? I told you!"

I whirled around and faced him. "But before you wet yourself with glee, let me point out that when you heard 'Arc-tic,' you started blabbering about ticks. Arctic has nothing to do with ticks either."

"Well, they sound the same."

"They're not the same. Arctic is a place, not a bug."

The treacherous little grin melted off his face.

"Oh rats. There for a second, I was so happy."

I paced over to him and laid a paw on his shoulder. "Cheer up, soldier. We've learned a lesson here. There's more to life than ticks and ducks. Both of us were wrong and we'll share the blame, fifty-fifty."

"I hate being wrong."

"So do I, but we can still find happiness."

He shook his head and sniffled. "I don't think so. I'm just crushed."

"Shhh. I've figured out a solution." I leaned forward and whispered, "We'll blame it on the cat!"

His eyes popped open. "Yeah, but he wasn't here."

"Well, that's a little inconvenient, but we can work around it. See, if the cat *could* have been here to make mischief, he *would* have been."

"Yeah, and you should never take a wooden nickel."

"Exactly my point. If we're going to pin this on the cat, we must ignore the tiny detail that he wasn't here. Don't forget, son, in the Security Business, we deal with larger concepts."

He gave that some thought and his grin returned. "You know, it might work. What a rotten little cat!"

"Exactly, and we're outraged that he made us look dumb, right?"

"Oh yeah, he won't get away with this!"

And with that, we sent our armored column to the house to find the cat. You'll love this next part.

CHAPTER THREE

Kitty's Plot
Blows Up

Is this exciting or what? You bet. Two brave dogs, filled with righteous indigestion and on the march to find Sally May's little crook of a cat. Wow.

When we rolled up to the yard gate, we stepped out of our Sherman tanks and surveyed the bottle of the battle...the bittle of the bottle. We surveyed the *field* of battle, there we go. All the people on the ranch were inside the house, eating soup. Hencely, there were no witnesses in the yard. Heh heh.

That was an important piece of combat intelligence because, well, Sally May rules the yard and takes a dim view of dogs who try to impose justice on her pampered, spoiled little crook of a cat.

She's a force to be reckoned with and we have to plan all our combat operations around her. See, she's equipped with the kind of radar that can pick up a naughty thought half a mile away and it's calibrated for dogs. We call her Radar Woman and it's no joke. When she switches on that radar, no dog is safe.

We have to scrub all the naughty thoughts out of our minds and slip into our Nice Doggie Disguise—which, by the way, doesn't always work. She's very suspicious and the woman can *read the mind of a dog.*

It's scary and kind of sad, to tell you the truth. I spend a lot of time worrying about our relationship. Sometimes I get the feeling that... well, she doesn't trust me.

But on this occasion, all the conditions looked good. I did a Visual Sweep of the entire yard and it turned up no signs of Sally May or her broom. It turned up no signs of Kitty Kitty either, but we knew he was lurking in the iris patch. He was too lazy to go anywhere else.

Data Control cleared us for the mission and I reached for the microphone of my mind. "Hank to Drover, over. We've got a Go For Launch."

"Oh goodie. Boy, I love soup."

"Negatory on the soup. We're cleared for

launch, not lunch. Over."

"Oh rats."

"Try to concentrate and keep up your morale. Remember, we're outraged."

"Oh yeah...wait. Over what? I forgot."

"How could you forget something that caused us to be outraged?"

"I don't know but I did."

"The cat."

"Oh yeah. The little scrounge! Wait. What did he do that made us so mad?"

There was a long moment of silence. "Drover, it's complicated. We have to trust our original sense of outrage and go from there. The point is that he's a cat. We're furious and want revenge."

"Oh, okay." He bared his teeth and made a growling sound. "How's this?"

"Looking good, soldier. Okay, listen up, here's the plan. This will be a quick strike, a rapid in-and-out situation. We'll charge over the fence, storm the iris patch, and run the little snot up a tree."

"This is so cool! I can't wait."

"Good. We need a brave volunteer to lead the charge and I was thinking...well, this would be a good time for you to build up your combat record."

"Me?"

"Yes, it's perfect. In and out, no major bloodshed,"

and plenty of glory in the aftermulch."

He glanced around. "What about Sally May?"

"She's busy inside, she'll never know."

At last he grinned. "You know what? I think I can do it!"

"That's the Drover we've all been waiting to see. Forward march, lead the charge."

"What about you?"

"I'll be with you almost every step of the way."

I would be with him in *spirit*, that is. Someone had to remain outside the yard to, uh, coordinate the mission. There was very little chance that Sally May would sniff this one out, but if she did...well, the runt would get some valuable experience. I'd gotten plenty of it.

His face bloomed into a dashing smile. "Okay, here I go!"

I watched as he...it was pretty comical, to be honest. I mean, he had no skills for breaching a barrier. First, he tried to clear the fence in one jump, the way I would have done it, but that flopped and so did he, hit the ground like a cinder block. Then he climbed and scrambled his way to the top of the wire and tumbled over into the yard.

"Great job, son, now do a Stealthy Stalk."

His Stealthy Stalk wasn't much better but at least he was moving along with the mission. He bunched up his body into the shape of a missile and crept toward the iris patch.

I heard a voice beside me. "My, my, what is he doing?"

"Shhh. He's on an important mission."

"Goodness gracious. Is he looking for the cat?"

"Yes. Mister Never Sweat. Shhh."

"Oh, you mean Pete?"

"Listen pal, we've got a very important…"

Huh?

I couldn't believe this. You won't believe it either. In fact, I'm not going to tell you, I mean, if something is unbelievable, we shouldn't believe it, right? So let's skip this and move along to another part of the story. I think it would be best for all of us, no kidding.

Oh well, you might have figured it out anyway. IT WAS THE CAT! Pete. Mister Never Sweat. He was sitting right there beside me and…oh brother. He was smirking, of course. He's always smirking and it drives me batty. He knows it drives me batty and that makes him even smirkier.

My mind tumbled. "What are you doing here, you little sneak?"

"Watching the big adventure, Hankie."

"You're supposed to be in the iris patch."

"Yes, well, I'm not. Sometimes I get bored and

walk around." He gave me a wink and whispered behind his paw. "We're coming to the good part, Hankie."

"What is that supposed to mean?"

"Watch this."

"Don't tell me what to do."

He shrugged. "Very well, don't watch this."

"I'll watch whatever I want to watch. I'm in charge here."

"Oh, that's right, that's right."

Since it was my ranch and I was in charge, I watched the whole thing…and once again couldn't

believe what I was seeing.

First off, the little pestilence climbed the fence and sprinted toward the house. There, he let out a blurd-cuddling squeech…a blood-curdling screech, that is, a screech that would have curdled your blood if you'd been there. We're talking about loud and piercing. Then he began limping around the yard, dragging his left hind leg and moaning as though he'd just been mugged. By a dog.

Oh brother. There wasn't one thing I could do about it.

Sure enough, I heard the thud of footsteps inside the house, then the back door opened and whacked against the side of the house—always a bad sign. Sally May emerged and she was mad when she got there. Her flaming eyes went to Kitty Invalid, the biggest fraud who ever lived, then her gaze speared ME, a totally innocent bystander.

Then came her voice. "Hank, what have you done to my cat!" She rushed over to the stupid cat and swept him up in her arms. "Poor thing!"

At that moment, Loper stepped outside. He was still chewing his lunch. "What is it?"

Her finger pointed at me like a poisoned arrow. "Him! Your dog is tormenting my cat. Again."

Loper blotted his lips with a napkin and glanced around. "Hon, Hank's not even in the yard. He's on the other side of the fence."

That threw some water on her flames and for a moment she didn't know what to say. "Well, I don't know how he did it, but I know he did."

Loper stepped off the porch and looked around. That's when he saw Drover, sitting near the iris patch, grinning like a monkey and wiggling his stub tail. "What about him?" He pointed to Drover.

Her mouth fell open. "Oh, my stars. He would never..." Her eyes darted back and forth. She set the cat on the grass and stormed over to Stub Tail. Bending at the waist, she shook her finger in front of his nose. "Naughty dog! Stay out of my yard and leave the cat alone! Scat!"

Drover's grin shattered and he followed her to the yard gate, moving like a worm. She flang open the gate and pointed her finger and entire arm to the west. "Out! And stop being mean to my cat."

Drover slithered through the gate and high-balled it to the machine shed.

While this was going on, Pete lounged in the grass, watched the show, licked his paw with long strokes of his tongue, and tried to control his laughter. I mean, here was a cat in his moment of glory, ready to take his bows in front of an audience of cheering admirers. It made me ill.

Sally May shut the gate, muttered something

under her breath, and started back to the house. As she approached Kitty Precious, he leaped up, took a stretch, gave me a wink, and fell in step beside her, gliding along without a hint of a limp, purring and wrapping himself around her ankles.

Oops. He tripped her and she almost fell. She stopped and looked down at him. You could see wheels turning inside her head. She looked at Loper, who had been watching. He grinned. "All at once, your cat looks pretty healthy."

She set her lips into a straight line. "Honestly. Between cats, dogs, kids, and cowboys, it's a wonder I have any marbles left." She bent down and gave Kitty a blast. "Go find something to do and stop tripping me!"

Wow! Humbled for the first time in years, Kitty fled to the iris patch. I wanted to bark my approval, but with Sally May, it's best not to push your luck.

I waited until she went back inside the house, then turned my gaze to the iris patch. I could see Kitty's ears mashed down on the top of his head, a sure sign that he was mad and sulking.

"Gosh, Pete, that one really blew up in your face. Thanks for the wonderful memories. You've done a great service for dogs all over Texas and I hope we can do it again sometime."

Hee hee! I LOVED IT!

CHAPTER FOUR

Drover Receives
the Weenie Award

Well, the Security Division had won a huge
moral victory over the cat and I was anxious
to share the news with Drover. Don't forget, he
had left the yard in tears.

Wait. That doesn't sound right. He hadn't "left
the yard in tears" because yards don't cry. Little
white dogs with stub tails cry. Thusly, we need to
say, "In tears, he left the yard." Now we're cooking.

I made my way up the hill to the machine
shed and was about to enter the slot between the
two big sliding doors, when something with
feathers and skinny legs came running up.

It was J.T. Cluck, the Head Rooster, and he was
out of breath. "Hold up, pooch, we've got things to
talk about. I've been looking all over for you."

"Well, here I am. I'll give you three minutes and I don't want to hear about your heartburn."

"Heartburn? How'd you know about that?"

"I know because that's all you ever talk about. You eat nails and tacks, they get hung in your gizzard, and you get heartburn. I don't care."

"Dadgum right, and big rocks will plug it up too. And stay away from spiders. They look tasty but they'll sure start a fire."

I might have mentioned this before, but J.T. had a ridiculous way of talking. He whistled his words, and when he said "Stay away from spiders," he sounded like a quartet of flutes.

"Do you suppose you could muffle your whistler?"

"Say what?"

"You whistle your words. It hurts my ears."

"Well, too bad. That's the way I talk. Do you want to hear this or not?"

"J.T., if you have something to say, get it out. The clock is running. "

"It's funny that you'd mention clocks. Them old wind-up clocks have springs and gears, don't you know, and one time I pecked up a gear. It wasn't big, just little bitty, but the darned thing got hung up and it sure gave me some heartburn."

"You're down to two minutes."

"Huh?"

"Get to the point, if you have one."

"Oh yeah." He glanced over his shoulders and leaned toward me. "Elsa's my wife."

"I know."

"She's a fine old gal but she takes spells. Now and then she gets a funny feeling in her bones, see, and it tells her that something awful's fixing to happen."

"Hurry up."

"Well sir, last night she woke me up and she was having one of them spells with her bones. See, when something awful is fixing to happen, she gets an achy feeling in her bones."

"Oh, I get it. This is another weather report. Everybody on the ranch is talking about an Arctic cold spell. I've already heard it, thanks." I started to leave but he stepped into my path.

"Naw, that ain't it. She don't do weather reports. This was something different."

I heaved a sigh. "Okay, you're down to one minute. Get to the point."

"I'm a-getting there, I'm a-getting there." He lowered his voice and moved closer. "Pooch, something bad's fixing to happen around here. Elsa thinks..." His eyes popped open and he let out a little chicken burp. "'Scuse me, it's all them ragweed

31

seeds. They're mighty tasty but you've got to watch 'em. They'll sure come back and bite you."

"What did Elsa say?"

"Huh? She said I was eating like a hog and I guess she was right."

"You said she was predicting something awful."

"Oh, that. Yes, Elsa's pretty sure that at ten o'clock tomorrow morning...THE SKY IS GONNA FALL!"

I gave him a shove. "You wasted my time to tell me that? Do you know how many times you and Elsa have predicted that the sky was going to fall?"

"Well now..."

"Ten times, twenty times. Every time your little chicken life gets boring, you start looking around for a catastrophe." I lowered my nose to the level of his beak. "J.T., the sky has never fallen. It's still there."

He looked upward. "Yes, but what's holding up all them clouds? That's the part that worries me. The longer they hang up there, the harder they're going to fall."

"Find something to talk about besides your heartburn and the sky falling. Get a job, go lay an egg. Goodbye."

I dived into the machine shed and heard him say, "Huh, I never thought of that. Might give it a try, sure might."

What a moron.

Well, I had to find Drover. The little guy had gone through a difficult time in the yard and I was pretty sure he would need some counselling. I looked under the work bench and didn't see him. That was no surprise. When he needs to flee from Life Itself, he goes to his Secret Sanctuary in the backest and darkest corner, where Loper keeps his canoe and Sally May stores her grandmother's furniture.

I moved in that direction, into the gloomy darkness. "Drover? I know you're in here."

I heard a faint voice. "No, I'm not here. I left."

"Where did you go?"

"Okay, maybe I'm still here but I'm never coming out. Sally May screeched at me and said I beat up her cat. I didn't even touch him! It just breaks my heart."

At last I found him sitting in the grandma chair, which was covered with a sheet. He looked sad and pathetic. "Drover, this has turned out better than you think. Pete was trying to work one of his schemes to get us in trouble, but it backfired on him. Sally May figured it out."

"Gosh, you mean..."

"Yes. Pete got into trouble and your mission

in the yard was a big success."

"No fooling?"

"Honest. In fact, you're in line to receive the Honor of the Golden Paw, a medal for uncommon bravery."

His eyes grew wide and he grinned, but the grin wilted. "Yeah, but I'm not uncommonly brave. I'm a little chicken."

"Drover, you've spent most of your life being a little chicken, but today you showed us something else."

"It was a mistake. I'm still a little chicken. I know, 'cause I live with me all the time."

I blinked my eyes. "So where do we go from here? Should we cancel the award for bravery?"

"Yeah, I wouldn't feel right about it. Everyone might expect me to be brave all the time."

"I hadn't thought of that. I guess we could give you the Weenie Award for being such a little chicken."

"That sounds more like it."

"Very well, step down and stand at attention." He hopped out of the chair and stood at attention. "By the powers infested on me by the so-forth, I bestow upon you the Weenie Award For Uncommon Chickenness." We didn't have any medals so I pressed my right front paw against his chest.

"Congratulations, soldier, we're ashamed of your chickenly behavior."

His eyes sparkled. "Gosh, thanks. It feels just like old times."

"Good, good. Well, let's move along. We have a lot of work to do to get prepared for the Arctic cold."

As we headed for the door, he said, "I hate cold. Are you sure they weren't talking about ducks?"

"They weren't talking about ducks."

"Oh drat."

Whew! What can you say? With Drover, we swerve from one loony situation to the next and there seems to be no end to it. I mean, who else *wants* to be awarded for being a little chicken? There's a kind of simple honesty in that, but you have to admit that it's pretty strange.

I've said it before and I'll say it again. He's the weirdest little mit I've ever mutted.

The weirdest little mutt I've ever mit.

The weirdest little...you see what he does to me? Let's change chapters and get out of here.

CHAPTER FIVE

The Cold Moves In

The impointant pork is that I had survived another conversation with Drover and we made it out of the fog of his Secret Sanctuary. We stepped outside into a day that had begun to change. Angry gray clouds had smothered the bright sunlight and a north wind moaned in the bare limbs of the elms and cottonwoods.

It was getting cold. It had nothing to do with ducks, and everyone on the ranch was getting prepared. Sally May and the kids had gone to town to pick up supplies. Loper and Slim had changed into heavy coats and winter caps. During lunch, they had caught the latest weather report on the radio: Winter Storm Warning. Blowing snow and days of deep, bitter cold.

Their long faces told the story: this was going to be a bad cold spell.

They spent part of the afternoon rushing to feed the cattle. See, cattle can survive brutal cold but they need some grub to keep up their energy and they also need water to drink. That was the biggest concern, water. Stock tanks freeze over in a cold spell and you have to chop holes in the ice.

The colder it gets, the thicker the ice. Nobody on our outfit wanted to find out how long a cow can survive without water.

When we finished feeding, the guys still had more work to do. They wrapped pipes with gunny sacks and set up a heat lamp in the well house at headquarters. They cut firewood and hauled one load to Slim's place and another to Loper's front porch.

The snow began falling around three o'clock. By six, it was drifting on the roads. We were back at headquarters by then and my guys were tired and hollow-eyed.

Loper said, "With these deals, we're always a step behind. You never think of all the things that can go wrong, but one thing's for sure. If anything can go wrong, it will when the temperature drops to zero."

"You've got frost on your mustache."

"And your nose is red." They smiled but Loper looked off to the north and his dark expression returned. "Sally May should have made it back by now. I hope they didn't have car trouble or hit a deer in the road. When you hit a deer, it blows the radiator and you've got no heater."

Slim nodded and turned up the collar of his coat. "In this kind of cold, you worry. That's a long old lonesome road. You want me to go look for her?"

"Let's give her another ten minutes. It's hard for her to get out of the grocery store without talking to people."

"I never had that problem."

Loper gave him a hard glance. "Well, you hardly ever go to the store and when you do, people look at what you've got in your shopping cart and know you're not normal."

Slim chuckled. "I've noticed that. A big package of turkey necks or chicken gizzards sure kills a conversation."

"Bachelors." Loper was glancing toward the north again. "I'd better go look for them. I won't have a minute's peace...wait, there's some headlights. It's her!"

Sure enough, Sally May and the kids had made it back home. She pulled up behind the house and the guys carried bags of groceries inside.

It was almost dark when they came back outside. Loper said, "Put some diesel treatment into your pickup and plug in the block heater. I'll call you in the morning and we'll come up with a plan for the day. It'll depend on the weather. Stay warm, if you can."

Slim had left his pickup running and it was nice and warm when we loaded up. We made a slow trip back to his house, driving through snow that was coming sideways in the north wind. In that kind of cold, the snowflakes were small and dry, blowing in swirls and waves through the beams of the headlights, and there were a bunch of them.

Drover was sitting up and staring straight ahead. I noticed that his eyes were crossed. "What's wrong with your eyes?"

His gaze drifted around to me. "Oh, hi. Yeah, it's everywhere."

"What?"

"Ice. It's everywhere. Ice and snow."

"No, I said 'eyes.'"

"Snow has eyes?"

"Drover, that's not what I said. Snowflakes don't have eyes."

"I didn't think so, but you said..."

"I said your eyes are crooked." He gave me an empty stare, so I raised my voice. *"YOUR EYES ARE CROOKED!"*

He flinched. "Don't yell, it hurts my ears!"

"I don't care about your ears. I'm talking about your eyes."

"I can't do anything about the ice. Slim's the one who's driving."

Speaking of eyes, mine had begun to bug out. I took several deep breaths and tried to calm myself. "Drover, can you hear me?"

"You're sitting near me?"

"That's not what I said."

"Your snot came out red? Gosh, maybe you've got a bloody nose."

"Drover, listen to me. I'll speak very slowly. Try to read my lips. Something...is... wrong... with...your...ears."

He frowned. "You know, I can't hear very well. Maybe something's wrong with my ears. They get plugged with wax." He hiked up his right hind leg and hacked on his right ear. "There, maybe that'll help. How's your bloody nose?"

"Listen, you little goofball, my nose is fine but your eyes were crossed. Your EYES"

"No, it was my ears."

"Your ears were not crossed. They were

41

plugged with wax and you couldn't hear me when I said that your eyes were crossed. Why were you crossing your eyes?"

He grinned. "Oh, that. I was trying to count snowflakes. Have you ever wondered how many flakes are in a storm?"

"No. I don't care how many flakes are in a storm."

"I've always wondered about it and I counted to umpty-eleven. I guess my eyes shorted out."

"Finally I get an answer and I'm sorry I brought it up."

"That's okay. I hope your nose gets better."

He hoped my nose got better. I stared at the little goof and felt my lips quivering. Was he trying to derail my thought processes or just being his normal weird self? It was hard to tell. I turned my back on him and watched snowflakes and went cross-eyed.

When we got to Slim's place, he parked the pickup beside the little building that served as his shop, saddle shed, and barn. He plugged one end of an extension cord into an electrical outlet and the other into a plug on the front of the pickup. He must have noticed that I was watching and wondering what this was all about.

"This is a block heater. When the temperature

gets below freezing, diesel engines don't want to start. You come out in the morning and your pickup's as dead as a hammer and you're afoot. The block heater warms the oil in the crankcase." He reached into the back of the pickup and brought out a plastic container. "This is diesel treatment. It keeps the fuel from gelling up in the cold."

He poured the diesel treesle into the fuel tank.

You know why dogs don't drive diesel pickups in the wintertime? First, they're too fussy and temperamental. The pickups are, not the dogs. Dogs are steady and reliable. We start ourselves every morning and we don't care how cold it is, and we don't need to drink diesel treesle.

The second reason dogs don't drive diesel pickups is that we don't drive pickups at all, so it would be pointless to...maybe this is obvious.

When we reached the porch, Slim gathered an arm-load of firewood and we headed for the door. As you might expect, Drover was shivering. "I'm f-f-freezing!"

"Well, look at the bright side. If you freezing now, just imagine what you'll be doing tomorrow morning when it's even colder."

"What's so bright about that?"

"I'm just trying to help, Drover. Me? I love the cold. It brings out all my savage instincts and..."

A blast of north wind took my breath away. It made me gasp and for a moment I couldn't speak. "It is cold, now that you mention it."

I threw a glance at Slim, who was squinting at the Dr. Pepper thermometer that hung on the porch post. "Ten degrees."

I configured my bodily parts to say, "Will you hurry up? We're freezing out here."

At last, he opened the door and Drover and I had a shoving match to see which one of us would be the first to squirt through the opening. I won but Slim tripped over me and dropped two sticks of firewood. Too bad.

Inside, he shucked off his big heavy coat and wool cap and dropped them in the middle of the floor. That was typical bachelor behavior, dropping clothes wherever they fell, and it would work out nicely for me.

I headed straight for the coat and went into the Digging and Fluffing Procedure. Slim growled, "Get away from my coat and make your bed somewhere else."

Fine. I didn't like his old flea-bag coat anyway.

He opened the door on the stove and shoveled the ashes of the morning's fire into the ash bucket. The fire had pretty muchly burned itself out during the day and he had to build a new one

from scratch. He started with crumpled-up pages
of *Livestock Weekly* and the Twitchell *Picayune*
and topped them with small twigs and pieces of
hackberry bark.

He struck a match, lit the paper, opened the damper, and watched the flames grow. He added small sticks, then chunks of cedar. He closed the door of the stove and adjusted the vent and damper.

He looked at me and said, "I like messing with a fire."

Good. Over the next several days, he would have plenty of opportunities to mess with his fire. His old house had a small propane wall heater in the bathroom and a gas cook stove in the kitchen, and the rest of the heat would have to come from his wood-burner.

I hoped he would take care of his business. We dogs expect a warm...wait, hold everything. Just then, something happened. It was so awful, so scary...sorry, that's all I can reveal at this point. You'll see.

A Mysterious
Coded Message

The scary part didn't happen right away but it will. Be patient.

Once Slim had tended the fire, he wandered into the kitchen, snapped on the light, and started looking for something to eat. Since he didn't invite me, I listened from the other room and tried to imagine what he was doing.

He opened a cabinet door and rattled through a collection of cans, then I heard the squeak of... what was that? Of course. He was opening a can of sardines, using the little metal key that came with the can. It made a certain squeaking sound that was usually followed by...yes, there it was, the smell of SARDINES.

Sardines produce a powerful rush of aroma,

don't you know, and it drifts into all parts of the house. All at once, my mouth was watering and I had to lick several drips off my chops. I cocked my left ear and listened and...yes, there it was, the crinkle of paper.

He had opened a package of saltine crackers, no question about it.

A chair scraped across the floor. He was now sitting at the dining table, eating sardines and crackers and probably reading whatever was written on the back of the cracker box, something exciting about crackers. I heard him crunch, chew, and swallow.

I could hardly bear the disappointment of not being invited to share in this important event, so I did what any normal, healthy American dog would have done. I went straight to his coat, which was still lying in a pile on the floor, exactly where he had dropped it, so I scratched around on it and flopped down.

It made a warm, soft, comfortable bed, and I felt that it would help me recover from the sting of being snubbed.

The coat didn't soak up all the pain but it helped, and before I knew it, I began drifting away like a little boat on a sea of molasses... snork murk snicklefritzzzzzzzz. I must have dozed off. Yes, I'm sure I did, I mean, that coat made a great bed, and the next thing I knew, a hacksaw voice was sawing on my eardrums.

"Hey, meathead, get off my coat!"

Huh?

Good grief, an angry man loomed over me like a storm cloud. And I smelled fish. The man appeared to be Slim Chance, not a fish. He grabbed the coat upon which I'd been whiching and gave it a jerk, spilling me across the cold floor, then he snarled, "Because of you, I'll have to hang it up." He flung open the closet door and hung my bed upon a peg. "What a waste of time."

He stormed over to his big easy chair and flopped down. Gee, what a grouch. I walked around the room, searching for a soft place to rest my poor bones. There were no soft spots, so I flopped down on a hard one. Ouch.

Slim covered himself with a wool blanket and was reading something, probably the Ranches-For-Sale section of *Livestock Weekly*. He did that with every issue and had been doing it for years and it made no sense. I mean, the guy was so poor, he couldn't have bought a bag of potting soil, much less a ranch. He was so poor, he survived on sardines and boiled turkey necks, and when he got engaged to Miss Viola, he gave her a lock washer instead of a ring.

But there he was, buried in his blanket and dreaming of all the ranches he couldn't buy. Oh well. It gave him something to do something on long, cold winter evenings.

Me? I was freezing on that hard, drafty floor. I tried to doze off and grab a little nap but...all at once, I became aware of a series of odd sounds. I lifted Earatory Scanners and homed in on...were they clicks? Yes, a series of clicks or clacks. Hmm, that was strange.

I shot a message to Data Control. "DC, we're picking up some odd sounds on our scanners. Is it random noise or something we need to check out? Over."

The radio crackled and DC came on. "Not random. There's a pattern. Could be the Charlies talking in code. Activate decoding procedures at once. Over."

"Roger that, DC, but we've got a problem. We've lost the code book. Over."

"Sorry, your session has expired. The next available session will begin in March. Offer not valid on Tuesdays or in Tennessee or to frogs under the age of thirty."

And with that, the line went dead. Oh brother. Frogs under the age of thirty? Sometimes I wonder why we bother with all this fancy technology.

Well, something had to be done about this. If the Charlies were out there in the dark, sending secret messages back and forth, we needed to bust their code and find out what was going on.

Have we discussed code breaking? Maybe not, because it's pretty complicated and highly classified. Very few dogs know beans about it, but when you rise to the position of Head of Ranch Security, they expect you to be effluent in codes, counter-codes, and code breaking. It's part of the job, so let's take a minute to go over some of the basics.

Okay, these new transmissions appeared to be in Boris Code, one of the toughest to desyphon. It consisted of a series of long and short signals, which we call "dots" and "dits." We write down the dots and dits on a special code pad, see, and make our best effort to transfume them into words and sentences.

Pretty amazing, huh? You bet. Okay, let's go to work on these mysterious transmissions and see what we can learn about Charlie's secret plans.

"Dit dot. Dot dit. Dit dit dot. Dot dot dit. Doo wah diddy. Diddy wump doodle."

Okay, there it was, the message in raw code that we'd pulled out of the aerosphere. Now we have to call up the Decoding App and work out the translation. Here we go, hang on.

"Oh, hi. This is Drover
and I'm f-f-f-freezing!"

Huh?

Freezing? Drover?

My eyelids drifted open. I blinked several times and noticed... hmmm. Had I been dozing? My assistant, Drover C. Dog, was curled up in a ball on the floor, shivering and clacking his teeth together. Do you suppose...

Ha ha. Boy, the mind plays tricks and we can call off the alert. Forget the secret codes. I must have drifted a little deeper into sleep than I thought. Ha ha. No big deal, it happens to dogs all the time, at least to those of us who work eighteen hours a day. The body gets worn out and begs for sleep.

See, those clicks and clacks were coming from Mister Shivers. The good news was that the Charlies weren't plotting an invasion of the ranch. The bad news was that we were freezing in Slim's house.

I leaped to my feet and went into the Shake, Yawn, and Stretch Procedure, then lumbered over to Drover and barked in his left ear. "Hey, wake up! You're clacking your teeth and disturbing the whole house."

Wow. He went off like a mousetrap, jumped

two feet in the air, came back down, and stared at me. Then he said—this is a direct quote—he said, "Buh buh...oh my gosh, where am I?"

"I'm not Bubba and you're in Slim's shack."

"Then how come my teeth are cracking?"

"Your teeth aren't cracking, they're *clacking*."

"What'll I do if they fall out?"

"Drover, pay attention. There's nothing wrong with your teeth except that they're clacking. You fell asleep and were clacking your teeth."

"Yeah, and that rhymes, so maybe the turnips can dance."

"What?"

His eyeballs quit rolling around and focused on me. "Oh, hi. Your teeth look better. Did you see all those turnips?" He tried to walk and fell flat, got up, and started scratching his ear. "You know, I think I might have been asleep."

"I think you might have been insane."

"Thanks, I knew it was something." He stopped scratching, glanced around, and started clacking his teeth again. "It's f-f-f-freezing in here, help, I c-c-c-can't control my t-t-t-teeth!"

Oh brother. The runt couldn't control his own teeth, for crying out loud, and...c-come to th-th-think about it, m-my t-t-teeth were starting to c-c-c-clack too. This was ridiculous. What's the point of being inside a house if you're freezing?

IT WAS TIME FOR SLIM TO CHUNK UP THE STOVE!

I swung my auditory devices around, took aim at Mister Wrapped In His Blanket, and cut loose with a blast of barking. "Hey! Your dogs are freezing. Stop mooning over all the ranches you can't buy, bring in some firewood, and warm this place up! If you don't, we will clack our teeth all night, moan, howl, whimper and shiver until the world looks level!"

Would it work?

His eyes appeared over the top of his paper. "What's eating on you?"

COLD! FREEZING!

"It seems a little drafty in here, don't it?"

No kidding. Duh.

"And the fire's died down. I reckon we could use some wood." He cupped a hand around his mouth and...you won't believe this part...he yelled, "Here, firewoods, here woodie-woodies! Come into the house, y'all, my dogs are getting cold!"

Oh brother.

He cocked his ear and listened. "Huh. They ain't coming."

Do other people behave this way around their dogs? I guess he thinks it's funny, but if you ask me, it's abnormal. The man is...something's wrong with him.

He flashed me a grin. "I guess I'll have to do it myself." He pushed himself out of the chair and shed the blanket, swished his sheepskin slippers across the floor and went to the window, where he could see the thermometer outside. "Good honk, it's two below zero! No wonder it seems cold."

At last, wearing nothing but his red one-piece long-john underwear and slippers, he threw open the door and crept out on the porch, leaving the door open. I heard him yell, "I'll be right back!"

Nobody would have guessed...well, you'll see. It's the scary part.

CHAPTER SEVEN

Slim Gets...DELETED (Classified)

Two below zero. No wonder we were freezing. This was the beginning of the Arctic cold front we'd been hearing so much about, and it still had nothing to do with ducks.

I could feel a cold breeze going through the house. See, a cold north wind will penetrate every little crack of an old house and Slim's shack had plenty of them, but who would have thought the door would blow shut?

Actually, it had a tendency to drift shut, even without a wind, because it was hung crooked, and the breeze inside the house just helped it along. Anyway, it blew shut. I didn't give it much thought, I mean, as long as the door knob wasn't set in the "locked" position, it was no big deal, right?

So I used this moment of down-time to scratch an itchy spot just below my right ear. Hairs flew in all directions and for a few moments, I enjoyed a state of pure bliss. I mean, unless you're a dog, you can't imagine how great it feels to answer a bad itch with a good scratch, and to disrupt the life of a stupid flea.

Wonderful! I hoped the little heathen suffered a terrible...

What was that? Did you hear something? Maybe not, because you weren't there, but I did because I was. I deactivated the Hacking Procedure and looked at Drover. "Did you say something?"

His gaze drifted back from deep space. "Oh hi. Did you say something?"

"Yes. I asked if you said something."

"I thought that's what I asked you."

"You did, but I asked first."

"I'll be derned. How come we're asking the same question?"

"I don't know."

"Maybe it has something to do with the moon."

"The moon? What does the moon mean?"

"That's a neat way to put it, 'What does the moon mean?'" He grinned. "And you know what? I just thought of a song. You want to hear it?"

"A song? At a time like this? You can't be

serious. Absolutely not." He wasn't listening and launched himself into a tiresome little piece of fluff and I had to listen to it. Here's how it went, in case you're interested.

What Does the Moon Mean?

I'm wondering what does the moon mean.
And what's in the gleam of a moon beam?
So many questions and not many answers
And maybe it's all just a dream dream.

What would we do if the moon moaned
Or what if it called on the telephone?
Mooning and meaning, streaming and gleaming,
Maybe the moon is not what it seems.

> Higgily piggily wiggly walk,
> The mouse ran up and down the clock.
> A quarter to seven or half-past eleven,
> And hickory snickory snock.

Maybe the moon means it's raining
Or maybe it just needs renaming.
A name is enough and clouds are a puff
To warrant a bit of retraining.

Maybe the moon is a feather.
That's why we're getting cold weather.
But whether it is or whether it's not
The weather is not what I'd rather.

Hi-lily, hi-lily, hi-lo, hi-lo.
Windy and cold and ice and snow.
It's freezing in here and so is my rear
I think that's all that I know.
I think that's all I know.

I was speechless. "Drover, where does this stuff come from?"

"I'm not sure, but did you like it?"

"No! It was...I don't even have words to describe it."

"Yeah, but everything rhymed. I love rhymes."

I felt my temper rising. "Drover, we don't have time for this. I asked if you heard something."

"Well, let me think." He rolled his eyeballs around. "You said my teeth were clacking and it kind of hurt my feelings."

"I don't care about your feelings and what I heard wasn't your teeth clacking. It was something else."

Just then, both of us heard it. It came from the front of the house and sounded almost as though…well, someone was trying to open the door…from the outside.

Drover's eyes grew as wide as saucers. "Oh my gosh, someone's trying to bust into the house! Robbers! Help!"

He was on his way to hide under Slim's bed but I blocked his path. "Take it easy, son, it's only Slim."

"Slim! What's he doing out there?"

I roasted him with a glare. "Maybe you ought to stop making up songs and start paying attention. He went out to get some firewood."

"He did? Oh good! It's f-f-freezing in here." The door knob squeaked and rattled but remained closed. Drover twisted his head to the side. "How come he's not coming inside?" The rattling continued, then we heard a loud clump, perhaps the sound of firewood hitting the porch. "Gosh, you don't reckon the door's locked, do you?"

"Rubbish. He never locks his doors."

Then we heard Slim's voice. "Holy cow, I'm locked out!"

Drover let out a squeak and began running in circles. "See? I told you! He's locked out and we're all going to freeze, help, murder!" He went sprinting down the hall and scrambled under the bed, the little goof.

I, on the other hand, went sprinting down the

hall and joined him under the bed, I mean, it seemed kind of silly, but in times of trial, a dog needs to do *something*.

We lay there in silence, listening to the sounds of our poor friend, tramping around on the porch, rattling the door, trying to open a window...and I began to realize that we weren't helping much, cowering under the bed.

I crawled out. "Come on, son, our pal's in trouble and needs our help."

"Yeah, but dogs can't open doors."

"Maybe we can't open the door but we can do the next-best thing."

"What's that?"

"We can BARK, Drover. When things fall apart, at least we can bark about it. Let's move out. Bring weapons and ammo."

We went streaking down the hall and into the living room. There, we established our Barking Line, faced the door, and started pumping out some BIG ONES, Number Three Lock-Breaker Barks. You should have been there to see us! Amazing. Two brave dogs fighting back against the creel, cool world.

The cold, cruel world, I guess it should be, and I don't know that we'd ever done a better job of barking. After three solid minutes of blasting, we were exhausted and had to take a break, I mean, we were out of breath and our throats were raw.

After refilling my tanks with carbon diego, I did a Damage Assessment and saw that...well, not much had changed. The door was still locked, Slim was still trying to figure out how to get back inside, the stove still needed wood, and the house was still cold. It was very discouraging.

I turned to Drover. "I don't get it. Those barks should have blown the door off its hinges. Were you taking careful aim?"

"Yeah, but by siduses are aggding ub on be and by dose is stobbed ub."

"That must have been the problem. You need to get your nose fixed."

"I wooden doe wear."

"You don't wear a wooden nose. It's an ordinary dog nose. It's not pretty but it shouldn't hinder your barking. Get it fixed."

He collapsed on the floor and started bawling. "I ked dalk whid by dose is stobbed ub and you're baking fudd of be!"

"Baking fudge? Listen, pal, Slim has never baked fudge in his whole life, and if he did, you wouldn't want to eat it. The problem is that he's locked outside in his underwear. Now shape up and stop blubbering."

He sat up and wiped his eyes. "Sorry. I'll dry harder negst tibe."

I stared at him and shook my head. "I have no idea what you said but at least you're not bawling. I guess that's progress."

"Thags."

You see what I have to put up with around here? I show up for work every day and try to do an honest job, but my assistant is a ninny who speaks Martian and makes up songs about the moon. It's a wonder the ranch hasn't fallen into ruins.

I began pacing, as I often do when it seems the only thing left to do. I could hear Slim outside, trying to pry open a window, and it seemed that he wasn't having much luck. That was bad news. If he couldn't pry open a window, he might have to...I couldn't even imagine.

In the meantime, Drover and I would be left alone in a cold house with a fading fire. We might turn into icicles and I would have to listen to him moan all night long.

I was in the midst of these dark thoughts when...hmmm...I began picking up some interesting signals on Noseatory Scanners. They had a foodish quality and, well, food is a very interesting subject if you're a dog.

I followed the trail of vapor into the kitchen and

had the scanners running full-blast. Sniff sniff. The vapor seemed to be coming from, well, the trash can and the closer I got, the smeller it was.

Fish. There was something fishy in there. I eased my nose over the edge and...oh my! Oh my my my!

SARDINES!

And you'll never guess what happened next. Hee hee.

CHAPTER EIGHT

A Gang of Big Rats

Maybe you'd forgotten that Slim had scarfed down a whole can of sardines for supper and hadn't shared even a bite with his dogs—his loyal friends, the Elite Troops of the ranch's Security Division. He hadn't even offered to let us lick the juice out of the can and that was shameful. We were starving.

Okay, we weren't starving. He had set out a double-handful of tasteless sawdust-and-grease kernels of Co-op dog food in the lid of an old shoe box. I guess that was his idea of Elegant Dining For Dogs: two scoops of buckshot served in the lid of a shoe box. And we ate it, of course. What's a dog supposed to do?

But with sardines, we're talking about eating

on a higher level, the kind of refined dining experience where taste and smell come together and form a...something. It's hard to explain. Maybe you have to be a dog to understand what the smell of sardines does to a dog's mind. When we catch a whiff of sardine juice, we begin thinking about things we wouldn't ordinarily do in a, uh, supervised situation, shall we say.

If you know anything about dogs, it isn't hard to figure it out what was fixing to happen.

I cast cunning glances over both shoulders. Slim was still out on the porch and I certainly hoped he didn't suffer frostbite, but this was providing me with a little window of opportunity, shall we say. It would have to be a quick job with no evidence left behind: paws on the rim, deep probe with the neck and head, snatch, grab, and run.

I rehearsed the opp in my mind, went over it several times. Yes, I could do it!

I hopped myself up on my back legs, rested my front paws on the edge of the trash container, plunged my nose into a month's-worth of Slim's kitchen debris, and ran a quick Garbage Analysis.

The GA gives us a profile of the owner's eating habits, don't you see, and it can be pretty revealing. Do we have time to take a peek at Slim's GA? I guess we can squeeze it in.

GARBAGE ANALYSIS OF SLIM CHANCE
Case #Pi-R-Squared 007
Pretty Secret

The evidence gathered in this analysis consisted mostly of empty cans, grocery store ads, coffee grounds, and the dried corpses of wasps, scorpions, and miller moths. Conclusions:

- *Subject shares the house with bugs.*
- *He doesn't read grocery store ads.*
- *He drinks coffee.*
- *He often eats out of a can.*
- *He doesn't wash out his sardine cans before disposing of them.*
- *Bad idea. The dogs will find them.*

End of Slim Chance Garbage Analysis
Please destroy!

So there's the book on Slim Chance, as revealed by his garbage. Pretty impressive, huh? You bet. Awesome. But let's get back to the sardine business.

I hopped my front legs onto the rim and leaned into...oops, the container fell over on its side and a few items spilled out on the floor. I took a glance over both shoulders, just in case Slim had blundered back into the house. All clear, so I moved into what we call a Toss

Procedure. It would require some digging.

I went to work with both front paws and bored a tunnel through the trash until I found it: a sardine can that still contained a deposit of fish juice, oil, and mustard sauce.

Wow! Bonanza!

I used my enormous jaws to lift it out and set it on the floor, then went to work. A sardine can is flat, don't you see, and doesn't weigh much, which means that…well, we have to chase it around the house, because every time we apply tongue pressure, it moves.

I chased it around the kitchen and then into the living room. By the time I reached the middle of the living room, my tongulary muscles were worn out. I was bushed and had to take a breather.

Drover was there. His empty gaze drifted down from the solar system and when he saw the can, his eyes lit up. "You found a sardine can?"

My tongue was so exhausted, I could hardly speak. "Yeth. While you were thtaring off into thpath, I wath doing an invethtigation."

"A what."

"An invethtigation."

He cocked his ear. "I can't understand what you said."

"I wath doing an invethtigation! What's wong

70

wiff you?"

"Oh, I get it. You did an investigation and found a sardine can." His smile wilted. "But you didn't tell me about it and I didn't get any and now I'm all upset. I never get to lick sardine cans!"

"Oh bwuvver. Wick the can and thtop whining."

"You really mean it? Oh goodie, I love sardine juice!"

He dived in and went to work on what I'd left in the can. It wasn't much but it brought a spark of meaning into his hollow little life. He licked and chased, chased and licked, all around the room.

I watched and, well, congratulated myself for being such a generous spirit, one who shared special events with his employees.

The fact that my tongue was limp with fatigue had almost nothing to do with it. Kindness and generosity were the main factors. No kidding.

Anyway, I gave my tongue muscles a break and watched Drover push the can all over the house. He was having fun and that was nice. Then I glanced back into the kitchen. Oops. It looked pretty bad. What had begun as a quick In-And-Out operation had turned into a big mess. Even Slim would notice.

At that very moment, I heard a window slide open. He was coming back!

To be honest, I had mixed feelings about that. On the one hand, I was glad he hadn't perished in the cold, but on the other hand...well, a dog could get blamed for such a mess and we needed to do a rapid Troop Withdrawal.

Drover was already highballing it down the hall to Slim's bed, a flash of terrified white fur moving at the speed of light. Zoom! I followed and seconds later, we were beeth blinkered boneath the bud...we were *both bunkered beneath the bed*, let us say.

There, we waited and listened. I couldn't see Slim, of course, and had to reconstroodle events strictly from Earatory Data. He crawled inside the house and closed the window and began making the kinds of chirps, mutters, and grunts you would expect from a man who was half-frozen.

He went to the closet and pulled on his coat and walked to the front door. There, he...well, he seemed to be speaking to the door. "That's all locks are good for, to keep a man shut out of his own house. Well, I'll fix you with a hammer and chisel and we'll see if you ever lock me out again. Dummy lock!"

He stepped out on the porch, gathered the arm-load of firewood he had dropped, returned, closed the door with a bang, and began rebuilding the fire. That took a while. Then his chair squeaked and his voice came down the hall.

"Hank. Come here."

Well, I was in deep trouble. I could tell by his voice. When he's half-mad, he roars. When he's seriously mad, he speaks in a voice that is calm, firm, and scary. That was the voice he had used to summon me.

Yes, I had been summoned. Maybe I would get a fair trial but probably not. Most likely, I would get tossed out into the ghastly frozen world and left to shiver and wither—all because of one measly sardine can.

That was the part that ripped me. If you're going to wreck a friendship, you ought to do it for more than a few slurps of sardine juice.

I crept out from beneath the bed, held myself erect, and looked down at Drover. "I must go. If I don't return, I want you to have my gunny sack bed."

"Yeah, but…"

"Good-bye, old friend." Holding my head high, I marched down the hall and presented myself to the Grand Inquisitor. "Here I am, sir. Carry out your duties."

He was wrapped in the blanket with nothing showing but his head. His eyes were…well, not what I had expected. They had a soft quality:

worried, concerned, even frightened.

"Hank, I caught a bad chill out there and I've got to raise my body temperature. Get up here and make a hand."

What! He wanted me to...no court martial, no lonely exile? Wow, what a deal!

I sprang into his lap and he covered us both with the blanket. I could feel his body shaking and hear him breathing: "Ka-ka-ka-ka!" The man had gotten a bad chill.

He wrapped me up in his arms and we began our Ritual of Sitting In His Lap. We had done it many times before and it was very special and maybe unique to a cowboy and his dog.

First, we looked into each other's eyes and he said, "Hi, Hankie." Next, he scratched both ears until my eyes sagged shut, then I burrowed my head beneath his left armpit and began uttering Groans of Bliss. When he scratched my ribs, I increased the volume of the groans and began pumping my right hind leg. This was...words can't even describe it.

I can't say how long it went on and maybe I dozed off, yes, of course, I mean, what else would a dog do under a blanket? I was awakened by a voice. Slim's voice. He had stopped shivering.

"Hank?"

Yes sir?

"While I was locked out of my own house and freezing my tail off on the porch…"

Gulp. Yes?

"…somebody went through my trash and made a terrible mess."

Oh. Yes. That.

"I think I know who done it."

Gulp.

"Did you happen to see a gang of packrats in here?"

What? Packrats?

"Big gray Norwegian rats with long tails?"

Ohhhhh! The packrats, a whole gang of them? Yes, by George, I did see them. There must have been a dozen…two dozen…hundreds of them.

"My guess is they were going after the juice in that sardine can."

Yes, exactly right. It was all coming back to me now. What a bunch of rats!

"Let's

try to keep that from happening again."

Roger that!

"I'll clean it up in the morning. Tonight, I want you in bed with me. You have kind of a fishy smell but you'll keep my bones warm."

He chunked up the stove with some big all-nighter logs and we sprinted down the cold hallway to the bed. I warmed his bones and we survived the night under three wool blankets. I also kept a close watch for that gang of home-wrecking packrats.

I'm proud to report that they didn't come back. They must have been pretty smart rats. They wanted none of ME.

Chopping Ice

I heard some kind of ringing sound. A telephone? Maybe it was a telephone, but I didn't have one in my office, so where was I? Someplace dark and warm. And there was a foot in my face.

A foot? That was crazy. Who...what...?

Then it all came rushing back. I had spent the night under the covers in Slim's bed. I heard him croak, "That's Loper calling." He threw off the covers and groped his way down the hall, in search of the telephone. "I'm coming, I'm coming!"

It was morning. I could hear the wind moaning and the house was frigid. I sprinted down the hall to draw some warmth from the stove, but the fire had died down and the stove was almost as cold as the house.

Slim stood beside the phone, hugging his arms for warmth. The floor was so cold, he had crumpled up his toes. He was wearing his red one-piece long-johns and his hair was in shambles. At his feet and all over the floor were the remains of...oops...last night's garbage caper. The packrats. Remember?

He said, "Loper, let me call you back. I need to chunk up the stove and get some heat in this house. Okay."

He hung up the phone and knelt beside the stove. He opened the stove door and used the ash scoop to pull the night's coals to the front. He made a little pyramid of newspaper, kindling, and bark over the coals and blew on them until they popped into flames. He added little sticks, bigger sticks, then logs.

He closed the door, adjusted the damper, went to the window, and looked out. Snowflakes danced and swirled in the wind.

He muttered, "The temperature's minus fifteen and the chill factor's probably thirty below zero. It makes a guy wish he had an inside job at the feed store."

He lit a burner on the kitchen stove and started warming his coffee water, pulled on his jeans and a heavy flannel shirt, and dialed Loper's number. "What's the plan? Okay, if I can get the pickup started, I'll be there in thirty minutes. And by the way, only crazy people go out in weather like this."

He boiled his coffee and poured it into a mug, then pulled on his heavy coat and wool cap with the ear flaps. He took a swig of coffee, spit out some grounds, and looked at the kitchen floor. "Boy, those rats sure made a mess. I'll clean it up later...if we survive."

I studied his face to see if...well, if he had figured out something about...you know, the rats. It was hard to tell, I mean he was pretty stone-faced in the morning, but he gave me a little grin that made me wonder.

But either way, we were still pals and that's all that mattered.

To nobody's surprise, Drover tried to remain in front of the stove but Slim flushed him out and off we went into...gag, that was the coldest wind I'd ever felt! It was the kind of wind that cuts to the bone and steals your breath away and makes your eyes water.

We ducked our heads against the wind and hiked down to the barn. Wait, hold everything and check this out:

- Arc-tic cold.
- Our ducks are cold.
- We *ducked* our heads against the cold.

Ducks and cold. Those clues had come up before and...never mind. Skip it.

First thing, Slim unplugged the block heater and here's why. If you forget and drive off with it still plugged in, it does bad things to plugs, sockets, and extension cords. If you show up at headquarters, dragging fifty feet of wrecked electrical cord, the boss will notice.

Slim had tried that once before and was determined not to do it again. He unplugged the block heater and we loaded into the pickup. He turned the key and the cold diesel engine growled and sputtered. When it finally started, it rattled and clanked and covered us up in a cloud of white smoke.

He let the engine run and warm up for five minutes, then we started down the snow-covered road to headquarters. It was making drifts on the south side of every fence post and tumbleweed.

When we arrived at headquarters, Loper was scraping ice off the windshield of his pickup, and his diesel was puffing out the same white clouds we'd seen on Slim's pickup. I guess you'd say it was the sign of a very unhappy diesel engine, one that hates to go to work on a bitter cold morning.

Loper was bundled up in his heaviest clothes and had a worried look on his face. "I dreamed about my banker last night."

80

"Brady? What did old Brady have to say?"

"He said that he and Lana were going to pay us a visit today. She's bringing a pitchfork and he's bringing a hot-shot, just in case they catch us hunkered around the stove."

Slim laughed. "Kind of warms your heart, don't it? If he brought a chopping ax, we could put him to work. You ever remember it being this cold?"

"It got down to twenty below when I was a kid, but we didn't have the wind. This is the worst I can remember, no-joke killer cold." He looked up at the gray sky. "In this kind of weather, machinery falls apart. We'd better feed with both pickups. If one breaks down or gets a flat tire, we won't have to walk back to the house. I hope we don't lose a bunch of cattle."

"If we can keep 'em in feed and water, maybe they'll ride it out."

"I hope so."

When he started walking toward his pickup, Slim yelled, "Hey! If you need some company, I'll rent you one of my dogs. I doubt that anybody else wants to ride with you."

Loper smiled. "Sure, I'll take Stub Tail. He's probably bored to death, hanging out with you."

I turned to Drover. "Okay, soldier, grab your gear. I'm assigning you to do Escort for the boss."

His gaze had been wandering. "Oh hi. Were you talking to me?"

"Ten-four. I'm splitting the force."

"Spitting on the floor?"

I gave him a snarl. "Don't start that again. I'm transferring you to another unit. You'll be riding Shotgun for the boss."

"Gosh, is that a promotion?"

"Yes, it's a huge promotion and you don't deserve it, but we're shorthanded."

His eyes flicked back and forth. "What'll I do?"

"Be alert and stay awake. If you see anything suspicious, bark at it."

And so it was that I sent the little mutt off on his first solo assignment. To be honest, it made me uneasy, I mean, I'd never had enough confidence to give him a Shotgun Job, all by himself. It was a big responsibility and involved considerable risk for the Security Division.

I hoped he was ready for it and didn't mess anything up. If he stayed alert and took care of the barks, maybe we would get through this difficult time.

The guys stacked twenty bales of alfalfa hay on Slim's flatbed and tied them down with ropes, then loaded sacks of feed in Loper's pickup. I supervised, freezing my hiney off in the awful wind. Drover watched through the window of Loper's pickup.

Off we went, driving through blowing snow to the pastures north of headquarters and honking the pickup horns. Our first problem was that in this kind of weather, cattle drift into canyons and ravines that give them some protection from the wind. They don't want to venture out, even for feed.

But they needed some propane to maintain their body heat. Wait, not propane. Protein. They needed protein to propane their body temperature, so we had to coax them out of their holes. We can't feed 'em if we can't find 'em, don't you see, and sometimes they can't hear the pickup horn in a high wind.

At last we located thirty snow-flocked cows hunkered down in a draw, with their heads hanging low and their tails facing the north wind. That sounds odd, doesn't it, their tails "facing" the wind. See, a cow's tail-end doesn't have a face. It has a tail. The cow's face is on the opposite end from the tail, so the point is...

Never mind.

We found them, is the point, and had some trouble coaxing them out, but we got 'er done. The guys threw off three bales of hay, cut the wires, and scattered it out so that all the cows would get a bite, then poured out two sacks of cake into the tracks the pickup had made in the snow.

The next thing the cows needed was water and that was the thing that worried Loper and Slim the most, keeping them supplied with fresh water. We drove to the stock tank and got to the fun part, busting ice on a thirty-foot stock tank. The cowboys called it "hard water," which was a kind of joke. The water was frozen, so it was *hard*, get it? Ha ha.

The windmill fan was spinning in the wind and pumping a stream of water that had made one little hole in a sheet of solid ice. Out came the axes and they went to work, one on the south end and one on the north. Axes chopped and chips of ice flew in all directions. They chopped and chipped, stopped to catch their breath, and chopped some more.

When they finally hit water, it splashed on their faces and froze. Loper had ice on his eyebrows and mustache, on the front of his coat and on the bill of his cap. Slim's glasses iced over so badly, he had to take them off and put them in his coat pocket.

After they'd busted holes in the ice, they got shovels and started scooping out the chunks. Those chunks gave us a look at the thickness of the ice, six to eight inches. That was some serious

ice, fellers. After making two holes, they sat down on the edge of the tank and caught their breath, which made fog around their faces.

This was the first of fourteen tanks on the ranch and the guys were already tired. I gave them a few barks to cheer them up. As they were about to leave, Slim looked down at the tank and said, "Good honk, it's already frozen again. By the time those cows get over here, it'll be solid ice again."

Loper heaved a sigh and shook his head. "They've got to have water. Let's drive 'em to the tank and chop it again."

So, with two tired cowboys afoot and one brave dog, we drove the cows to the tank. (Drover watched from the pickup, of course). Once the cows reached the tank, they tried to drink but couldn't, so the boys busted the ice again and the cattle finally got their drink. They were thirsty.

We drove on to the next pasture. This time, and for the next three days, we fed the herd right beside the tank. While the cattle ate their hay and cake, the guys chopped holes in the ice. The cows had about ten minutes to grab a drink before the holes closed up solid.

This was not a fun time to be working on a ranch.

CHAPTER TEN

The Blue Jean Queen of North America

W e made it through the day and at six o'clock, we were back at headquarters. We'd done all we could do.

My guys were worn out. They hadn't stopped for lunch, just kept going on beef jerky and raisins, and never turned off their diesel pickups. In that cold, you didn't dare shut one down because you might not get it started again.

We were standing in front of the machine shed. Loper rolled a kink out of his shoulder. "It's going to be worse tomorrow. It's supposed to drop to fifteen below zero again tonight. That ice might be a foot thick in the morning."

"Why don't you call Brady and tell him to come get his cows?"

Loper managed a chuckle. "He'd shoot me first but he'd save back a load for you."

"Is it too late for me to turn in my two-week's notice? I was thinking it might be a good time to set up a snow cone stand on South Padre Island."

"You know what? This cold goes all the way down to the Gulf. It's five degrees in Austin and they're losing electricity. It's a wreck."

"How'd you know that?"

"Radio. You ought to try it sometime. Do you have enough firewood?"

"I'll burn what I've got and then start busting up the furniture. A country boy will survive. And I've got my electric blanket."

"You've got an electric blanket?"

"An electric dog, I guess it should be." He looked down at me. "Old Hankie kept me warm last night."

Huh? Everyone was looking at me, so I squeezed up a smile and went to Broad Swings on the tail section. A dog needs to grab these tender moments and make the best of them.

Loper took a deep breath and let it out slowly. "Man, I'm tired and tired of being tired and tired of being cold. Maybe we'll make it. We'll see what it looks like in the morning."

He shuffled down to the house and we headed for

Slim's place. He parked the pickup beside the saddle house, shut off the motor, and plugged in the block heater. We hiked up to the house and I noticed that the porch light was on. We had left in the dark and were coming home in the dark. Long day.

On the porch, Slim stomped the snow off his boots and gathered an armload of wood and we went inside. It was good to be home. The house was warmer than the porch but not pleasant. Slim guessed 45 degrees.

He lit the oven and left it open a crack, so that it would start warming the house. He walked past the, uh, debris from last night's garbage caper and didn't say a word about it. The man was tired.

He went to work rebuilding the fire in the wood-burner. When we'd left the house that morning, he had filled the firebox with chunks of hardwood but in the afternoon, it had died down to coals. A fire in that stove lasted about five hours. That's why the house seemed cold. It was.

Slim flopped down in his big easy chair, didn't take off his coat or hat or boots, just flopped down. His eyes slammed shut and within minutes, he was snoring. Not me, fellers. Somebody on this outfit had to...okay, maybe I drifted off too.

I hadn't worked as hard as Slim, for the simple reason that dogs don't chop ice, but I had put in a long hard day, so...yes, I admit that I followed Slim's example and started pushing up a line of Zs.

But let me hasten to add that Drover fell asleep before I did.

Supper? There would be no supper. The word wasn't even mentioned.

I don't know how long I slept, but something woke me up, some kind of noise. My head leaped up and so did my ears, then my eyes popped open. We're talking about the Full Alert Configuration on all instruments.

I blinked my eyes and glanced around. Nothing fit together or made sense. I reached for the microphone. "Unit One to Drover, over. Report to the office at once and pass the biscuits."

After a moment of deadly silence, I saw the outline of his outline, sitting up, weaving back and forth, and his eyes were crooked. "Did someone call me?"

"Roger that, affirmative, yes. Something's going on around here. Did you hear an odd sound?"

"Well, let me think."

"It was a tapping sound. We may have peckerwoods pecking on the wood."

"I thought it was a biscuit."

"No. We're talking about wood."

"Which wood?"

"The house is made of wood and the peckerwoods are trying to eat it."

"Yeah, but it's winter and they all went south."

"Why wasn't I informed? How can I run this ranch when the birds don't turn in their reports?"

"Beats me." He yawned and glanced around. "Gosh, where are we?"

"I have no idea. Wait. We're in Slim's house and we've got whickerbills pecking on the woodchucks. Load up Number Three Warning Barks and commence firing."

We formed a line and began blasting out the Number Threes. Those are the big ones, don't you know, with a recoil that will throw a dog backwards on every blast. At that stage of the operation, we didn't know exactly where to aim the barks so we did a Spray Pattern, in hopes that we'd hit something out there.

I don't know if we hit anything but we got Slim's attention. He came flying out of his nap and yelled, "Knock it off! Someone's at the door."

Huh? The door?

Okay, we called off the alert. Ha ha. False alarm. See, Slim had a front door on his shack and, just as I had expected, somebody was knocking on it. You might have thought it was peckerwoods pecking on the wood, but that would be incorrect.

But who would be knocking on Slim's door on

a night like this? We couldn't blame it on the cat. He was two miles away, smirking and purring in Sally May's warm cozy house, the little sneak.

Oh yes, he had weaseled his way into the house and maybe I forgot to file that report. Back at headquarters, whilst Loper and Slim were talking in front of the machine shed, I happened to glance toward the house and saw...this is the part that burned me up...I saw the pampered little snot, sitting in the window.

Yes, it was Pete and, naturally, since he was inside a nice warm house and I wasn't, he took his smirking to an even higher level. While wearing that disgusting smirk all over his cheating little face, he waved a paw at me and STUCK OUT HIS TONGUE!

Well, you can imagine the effect that had on me (bad, explosive) and that's why I didn't mention it. I didn't want to create the impression that he drives me batty, but he does and now everybody knows.

The little creep. One of these days...

But the point here, the moist impointant point, is that somebody was knocking at Slim's door on the coldest, darkest night of the year, and we couldn't blame it on the cat. There. We got that out of the way.

Slim went to the door and opened it. I leaned forward and studied the scene. It appeared to be someone wearing an overcoat and a furry hat...a lady, perhaps, with rosy cheeks and a pretty smile and...holy smokes, THAT WAS MISS VIOLA!

My jaw dropped and my eyes bugged out, and the same deal happened to Drover and Slim. All three of us sat there like frogs on a log, bug-eye and drop-jawed, staring at the cutest, sweetest gal in Ochiltree County.

She smiled and it lit up the whole world. "I hope I'm not interrupting something." Slim couldn't speak and might have swallowed his tongue. "May I come in? It's cold out here."

At last he found his voice. "Oh, shore, shore, come on in."

She came inside and Slim closed the door. Her gaze skipped around the house and stopped on the...oops. Don't forget, Slim hadn't gotten around to picking up the you-know-what. She didn't say anything but she saw it, first thing.

"Viola, what in the cat hair are you doing, driving around on a night like this?"

That's when we saw the cooking pot. She held it up. "I thought you might enjoy a hot meal. Have you eaten supper?"

"Ha. I don't even remember the last time I ate."

"That's what I figured. Daddy was caged up in the house all day and made a big pot of his special venison stew and wrecked the kitchen. I haven't tried it, but it smells delicious. I'll put it on the stove to warm." She took the pot into the

kitchen and returned, picking her way around the, uh, debris. "Is this a new decorating idea?"

He laughed. "You notice every little thing."

"Little? Ha!"

"A pack of wolves broke in last night. I'll clean it up one of these days. I ran out of energy. It was a hard day on this outfit."

She sat down and he told her about our day in the cold, snow and wind.

Now that she was sitting, I seized the opportunity to, well, snuggle, shall we say. I inched my way over to her chair and rested my head in her lap. Hey, what kind of dog would pass up a deal like that? Not me. I mean, this was the Blue Jean Queen of North America and she deserved a chance to stroke my ears.

She did and, oh! All the pain and suffering of the day just melted away. All at once, it didn't matter that the world was harsh and cold or that the cat had weaseled his way into Sally May's warm house. All that mattered was that I had Miss Viola and she had me!

Wow!

And so it was that we ran away to a castle in the Alps and lived happily ever afterly, and that's the end of the story.

CHAPTER ELEVEN

Oh no!

Okay, it wasn't the end of the story and that deal about us running away to a castle didn't happen. Viola was crazy about me but don't forget that she was engaged to Slim Chance and wore his engagement ring with the microscopic diamond.

That was kind of a bummer but I tried to make the best of it. See, whilst she was listening to Slim's tales of busting ice and saving the lives of hundreds of cows, I managed to lay a paw on her lap...then another, then...this is impressive, so pay attention...I oozed my entire body into her lap.

And there I was, in the very spot where every dog in Texas wanted to be. It was one of the most glorious moments of my whole career.

Slim was still talking. "What I'm worried

about is losing electricity. If we lose power in the night, we'll lose the block heaters and our diesels won't start. We'll have three hundred cows shivering in the cold, without water and feed." At that moment, he noticed me. "Hank, for crying out loud, get out of her lap and leave her alone."

I pressed myself against herself, tapped my tail, and looked up into her adoring eyes. She smiled! See, what did I tell you? She was nuts about me...huh? She more or less eased me back onto the floor and stood up. Rats.

"I need to be going anyway."

"What? You just got here. You might as well stay for supper."

"Daddy said if I wasn't back in thirty minutes, he'd come looking for me."

Slim grumbled and rose from his chair. "Well, that would be cute, you and Woodrow out in the dark on the worst night of the year. Then I'd have to go looking for both of you." He put his arm around her shoulder. "Thanks for the supper. I really appreciate it."

"You're welcome and I hope you enjoy it." She pulled on her gloves and turned up the collar of her coat. "It seems cold in this house."

"It is cold. In this kind of weather, I have to keep the fire going. Last night, I went out for stove wood and the door blew shut and locked me out."

She stared at him. "You were locked outside? In this bitter cold? Slim, that's terrible! People die in this kind of weather."

"Well, I pried open a window and got back inside, so you won't have to go to a funeral this week—not mine, anyway."

"Slim, we have a spare bedroom upstairs and you'd be welcome..."

"I wouldn't do that to Woodrow. He'd probably move out in the yard and then we'd have to go to his funeral. I'll be okay."

She gave her head a shake. "Honestly. I have to figure out how to live with two mules." She started to leave but paused. "Oh, he wondered if you have a backup generator."

Slim grunted a laugh. "A backup generator? No. Loper's too cheap to buy one and I have to admit that he's got a point. Those generators sit in the barn for five years and by the time you need it, the carburetor's gummed up and it won't start. On this outfit, we depend on dumb luck and divine guidance."

"Well, I hope it works." She waved goodbye to me and went out into the cold. Okay, maybe she waved to all of us but mostly to me. She certainly didn't mean it for Drover.

Slim stood there for a minute, thinking. "Boy, that's a fine lady. And she brung me a big pot of stew, just what I need." That put a little spring into his step and he headed straight for the kitchen.

The smell of stew had filled the house and it smelled delicious. I didn't have much hope of getting any of it, but a dog has to stay open for business, even when the prospects don't look good. We survive on the hope that there's more to life than Co-op dog food.

I followed him and set up shop beside his chair at the dinner table.

He managed to find a bowl and a spoon in his bachelor kitchen and sat down. "The Lord knows we're grateful," he said, and dug in. "Oh yes! Mighty tasty. Carrots and taters." He gave me a wink and chewed on a hunk of venison...and chewed...and chewed.

He pulled it out of his mouth, studied it, and pitched it to me. Snap! He tried another hunk of meat and...same deal. He chewed and chewed and chewed, I mean, I could hear his jaws popping.

He pulled it out of his mouth and looked at it. "That's either the oldest buck deer in the Panhandle or a boiled owl."

He pitched it to me and I nailed it. Snap! It never had a chance to hit the floor. It was pretty tough, but on a job like this, we cancel Chews and go to Gulps. Drover must have heard the action and showed up.

We polished off the first batch and Slim went back for seconds, and the three of us spent a very pleasant half-hour, working on Woodrow's stew.

It turned out to be a very productive evening for us dogs, and Slim seemed satisfied too, but he spent about ten minutes picking his teeth with a sliver of firewood. He said, "I ain't had so much meat in my teeth since I tried eating a jackrabbit."

That was our evening's entertainment, eating Woodrow's venison stew and watching Slim pick his teeth. It was fun but we all noticed that the house was cold, even though the stove was burning full-blast. Outside, the wind howled and groaned, and we could feel a breeze blowing across the room. The curtains were moving.

Slim went to the window and looked out at the Dr. Pepper thermometer. "Good honk, twelve below zero, and there's no telling what the chill factor is. Boy, if we lose power..."

There wasn't much left for us to do but go to bed, but the bedroom was so cold, Slim dragged his blankets into the living room and made his bed in the chair. It was closer to the stove, don't you see, and he knew he'd have to get up in the night to punch up the fire.

He was still wearing his coat. He'd never taken it off.

He climbed into his chair-bed and said, "Come on, pooch." I jumped into his lap and he wrapped us up in wool blankets. Drover curled up in front of the stove and shivered.

Oh, here's one little detail you probably missed, since you weren't there. Slim turned off all the lights in the house except the one in the kitchen. I noticed but didn't think anything about it until later. You'll see.

I had just about drifted off into a sweet dream when I heard Slim's voice. "Hankie, remember that song I told you about yesterday morning? I had the title but no words. Well, I've got it all put together. You want to hear it?"

I couldn't believe this. What was going on around here? Everybody in the house wanted to sing me a song and all I wanted was a good night's sleep. Well, I was trapped and had no choice but to listen, and if I have to suffer through it, so do you. Let's get it over with.

When I Tried to give My Dog a Job, He Couldn't Stay Awake

This story began in the winter on a cow
ranch north of Amarillo.
Me and old Hankie was batching together
in a shack on the banks of Wolf Creek.
The weather turned cold, and boys, it was
wicked, that north wind was packing a
knife.
Regardless of that, we had us a job taking
care of a bunch of hungry cattle.

The morning was gray and colder than snot
when we started our day of work.
The diesel pickup was crabby and cold and
didn't want to fire up.
But we loaded our feed and set out like heroes
in the snow on the Wolf Creek Road.
I hoped that old Hankie would help with the
driving, but he fell asleep sitting up.

Now, slacking a duty's a no-no, it's
something a cowboy won't take,
But when I tried to give my dog a job, he
couldn't stay awake.

103

It kindly hurt my feelings that my partner
  had quit me like that.
It made me wonder if I was so boring it
  caused his eyes to slam shut.
But what about Lassie and Yukon King and
  them other dogs in the movies?
They was brave and heroic and never fell
  asleep when their master was needing
  their help.

  Now, slacking a duty's a no-no, it's
    something a cowboy won't take,
  But when I tried to give my dog a job, he
    couldn't stay awake.

I had the pickup in four-wheel drive and kept
  'er going down the road.
But I kept a close eye on my buddy while I
  was fighting the ice and the snow.
His eyelids were fluttering like wings on a
  June bug, he was snoring like a couple of
  mooses.
I said, "That's enough" and slammed on the
  brakes and throwed him right into the
  dashboard.

  I think it delivered a message, that

slackers can jump in the lake.
Next time I give old Hankie a job, he'd
    better stay awake.
Next time I give old Hankie a job...he'll
    fall asleep, like he always does.

He finished the song and a deep silence moved over us. "What do you think, pooch? I sent it to my agent and he loves it. If it catches on in Nashville, you'll be a famous dog."

A famous dog. Oh brother. It was, without a doubt, the dumbest...you know, he thinks his songs are funny but they're NOT. They are so corny...never mind, but if dogs wrote the history books, a lot of people wouldn't believe what goes on in the Wild West.

We finally drifted off to sleep. Slim got up several times in the night to chunk up the stove, just what we'd expected, but then...it must have been around daylight. Yes, the house was mostly dark but a sliver of gray light was showing in the east.

I had tumbled into a pretty serious state of sleepinghood and was enjoying a nice dream about...something, maybe bones or venison stew, when things started falling apart.

Slim's voice boomed like a clap of thunder. "Holy cow, the power went out!" He bucked me out of the chair and threw off the covers. When I hit the floor, I still had minnows swimming through my head but managed to figure out why he'd left the light on in the kitchen: *so he would know if the electricity had gone off in the night.*

And it had!

He'd slept in his clothes, so it didn't take him long to get ready. And fellers, he was moving at a high rate of speed. Ordinarily, he wasn't much of a sprinter in the early morning, but today he was rattling his hocks. I was still a little groggy but followed him out the door. (Drover stayed inside, of course).

GAG! The sky was clear and the sun was out, but that wind had a razor in it. For a second, I couldn't breathe for a second. Slim ran north, straight into the wind, and I followed. He seemed to be heading toward...of course! The pickup.

When the power went out, we'd lost the block heater and he wanted to start the engine before it went stone cold.

When we reached the pickup, he couldn't get the door open. It was frozen shut. He got a shovel out of the back end and pried it open. His hand was shaking when he turned the key. He cocked his head and listened as the motor said... rurr rurr...rurr...silence.

That told the story and he turned off the key. "Too late. We're busted, dadgum the luck! Busted and afoot and as worthless as a bunch of sheep." He set his lips in a tight line and was quiet for a moment. "I'd better call the boss...if the stinking phone ain't out too."

CHAPTER TWELVE

It Looks
Pretty Bad

We hiked back to the house. Slim gathered an armload of wood on the porch, took it inside, scooped the ashes out of the stove, and rebuilt the fire. When he had a good blaze going, he closed the stove door and set the damper.

As you might have guessed, Drover had slept through the entire drama. Now he was sitting as close to the stove as he could get without going up in flames. His teeth were clacking. "It's f-f-f-freezing in here!"

"Yes, and you're hogging the stove. Move over." I gave him a shove and took the best spot, right in front of the air vent on the stove door. It felt wonderful, perfect, and I deserved it.

After a moment, Drover said, "I smell

something burning."

"Yes, there's a fire in the stove. When fire burns, it smells like a burning fire."

"No, it smells kind of like...hair."

"Stoves don't have hair, so it follows from simple logic...YEOWWW!"

Never mind. Nothing happened.

Where were we? Oh yes, Slim removed his gloves and stood in front of the telephone. He looked at it for a moment and licked his lips, then picked up the receiver and put it to his ear.

"Well, it's got a dial tone. Here we go." He dialed a number and waited. "It's ringing." His brows jumped. "Loper? It's me. My power went out in the night and I've got a dead diesel. If you can get yours started, maybe we can use jumper cables...oh great. I was hoping...well, we're skunked."

He hung up the phone and stared at the floor, then walked to the front window and looked outside. Have you figured it out? Loper had lost power too and neither pickup would start in the cold, so nobody would be feeding cattle or chopping ice...ice that was getting thicker by the minute.

It looked bad. It looked very bad. Do we dare go on with the story? There's no telling what might happen. It could get scary and sad, and you know me, I worry about the children.

What do you think?

Are you sure?

Okay, we'll mush on and see what happens. Hang on to something solid.

Things had turned about as gloomy as they could get. The electricity had gone out, neither pickup would start, the cattle had no water, and Drover and I were trapped inside a cold house with a restless, unemployed cowboy who would spend the whole day pacing from window to window and muttering to himself.

That's what he does, you know. If the cattle are suffering, he must suffer too. If the cattle are miserable, he has to be miserable right along with them, and inflict all the misery and suffering onto the dogs.

And to make things worse, I had scorched a patch of hair on my back and it would probably become a bald spot and I would look like a freak for the next month.

It was going to be a long, awful...huh? Wait a second. I heard something and so did Slim. A droning sound. He looked out the window. "Good honk, is that...I ain't believing this. It's Woodrow! What is that old goat up to now?"

He leaped to the door and I was right beside him. (Drover slithered underneath the coffee table and hid, the little weenie). We plunged outside, into the wind and cold, and headed for the pickup that was now parked beside Slim's piece of junk.

When we got there, the old man had just let down the tail-end gate of his pickup. He was wearing insulated coveralls, a big parka with a hood, and his usual sour expression. In the bed of the pickup we saw...hmm, was that a generator? Yes, a five-kilowatt gasoline generator on skids.

Woodrow didn't bother with chatter. "Grab the other end and help me unload this thing."

It was heavy. "How'd you get it loaded?"

"Tractor."

That was the end of the small talk. Woodrow grabbed the starter rope, pulled it twice, and the generator started chugging. He plugged the extension cord into the generator which...I don't know, activated the block heater on the pickup, I suppose. Yes. They were going to warm up the motor so it would start.

Without a word, Woodrow unrolled another extension cord, plugged it into the generator, and hooked the other end to...some device. "Open your pickup hood."

Slim popped the hood and raised it. Woodrow switched on the device (it made a whirring sound) and pointed it toward the diesel engine.

Slim yelled, "What is that?"

"My daughter's hair dryer."

Slim shrugged his eyebrows and watched. "How'd you manage to get your pickup and tractor started?"

"I change my fuel filters once in a while. Filters collect water. Water freezes." After a bit, he told Slim to crank his pickup. He tried but the battery was drained.

Woodrow handed him the hair dryer. "Hold it on the fuel pump." He opened the hood of his pickup and hooked up a set of booster cables to Slim's battery. "Now try it."

Slim scooted into the seat and gave it a crank. Rurr rurr rurr...then it fired and started, chug chug rattle rattle clank, and puffed out clouds of white smoke.

Slim was thrilled. "Hey, we're back in business! Nice work, Woodrow."

The old man was busy. He disconnected the jumper cables and slammed his hood. "Help me load this thing." They lifted the generator into the bed of Slim's pickup. "You got jumper cables to start Loper's rig?"

"Yes sir."

'You'll need this." Woodrow handed him the hair dryer. "Ice is too thick to chop. Use a chainsaw."

"Thanks for the generator...and the stew."

"Change your fuel filters." He got into his pickup and left.

Slim chuckled and shook his head. "Old Prince Charming. 'Change your fuel filters.' Come on, pooch, let's go rescue the boss."

Well, old Woodrow had turned things around in our little world and they started getting better. The temperature was still below zero, but the sun was shining and, most important, the wind had slacked off. That helped a bunch.

At headquarters, we went through the same routine with Loper's pickup: generator, block heater, hair dryer, and jumper cables. The diesel didn't want to start but it finally did, with a lot of clanking and puffs of smoke.

We loaded feed in both pickups and were ready to go north. Slim said, "Here's an idea. Why don't we use a chainsaw to cut the ice?"

Loper stared at him. "We've got axes and strong arms. We don't need a chainsaw."

"Let's throw it in, just in case."

Loper grumbled and rolled his eyes. "America is going soft."

Slim loaded the chainsaw into Loper's pickup.

At the first tank, the boys chopped for twenty minutes and ice chips were flying around like starlings. Loper stopped and caught his breath, which came in clouds. "Where'd you get the idea of using a chainsaw?"

"Old Sourpuss."

He sighed. "Give it a try."

Slim got the chainsaw, fired it up and used it to cut the ice into blocks, then they pried them out with shovels. The cattle rushed to the water and slurped it up before it froze solid again.

Loper watched them drink. "That old man is pretty shrewd."

"When you're as grumpy as he is, you have to be shrewd. And this ain't his first rodeo."

By the end of the day, all the livestock on the ranch had feed and water. The boys were in a better mood and so was Sally May. The electricity had come back in the afternoon. I'm sure her cat enjoyed getting his house warmed up.

Around dark, when we got back to Slim's place, we saw Woodrow's pickup parked out front and Slim muttered, "Uh oh, he's back."

But it wasn't Woodrow. Out stepped the Blue Jean Queen of North America, wearing her furry hat and her sunshine smile that melted all the ice for miles around. Drover went into such a swoon, he fell off the pickup seat. Me? I tried to dive out the window but the glass was rolled up. Ouch.

Viola had brought us a pot of chili—made by her, not Woodrow, with real beef, not road-kill venison. "Slim, I ate some of that stew for lunch and…I'm so embarrassed! It was like eating an old tire."

Slim laughed. "We have to do something with those old tires. I guess that's why God made toothpicks."

"Well, I'm glad you can see the humor in it, but the next time Daddy decides to play chef, I'll feed it to the coyotes."

Slim enjoyed another chuckle. "Thanks for the chili. I'll put it to good use. And I really appreciate your dad bringing the generator. Tell him we tried his idea of cutting ice with a chainsaw and it worked slick."

"He'll be pleased. Sometimes it's hard to tell, but he likes you." She smiled and blew us a kiss and drove away into the night, leaving all three of us tingling and sparkling and wishing…

Slim said, "Somebody needs to marry that gal."

I stared at him. Yes? What about that? He certainly wasn't waiting for his dogs. We would have swooped her up long ago and if he didn't hurry…

Oh well, we'll leave that for another story. We'd made it through the Incredible Ice Event and this case is…

Wait, one last thing. Whilst Mister Pampered

116

Kitty was loafing inside the house, he tried to sharpen his claws on Sally May's couch. Hee hee. That caused a major explosion and he got moved to the tool shed, where he sulked and whined for two days. The little snot.

I loved it. When the cats are unhappy, life is good! Now we can say it...this case is closed.

Have you read all
of Hank's adventures?

Finding Hank
The Most-Often Asked Questions about Hank the Cowdog

For more than 35 years, John R. Erickson has entertained three generations of readers with Hank the Cowdog's hilarious antics, and now, for the first time, in this beautiful, full-color volume, he answers the most common questions he has received from fans over the years!

Written in an engaging question-and answer style, this collector's item — complete with illustrations and original photographs — provides a unique behind-the-scenes look at the people, places, and real-life animals and incidents behind your favorite Hank stories!

And, be sure to check out the
Audiobooks!

If you've never heard a *Hank the Cowdog* audiobook, you're missing out on a lot of fun! Each Hank book has also been recorded as an unabridged audiobook for the whole family to enjoy!

Praise for the Hank Audiobooks:

"It's about time the Lone Star State stopped hogging Hank the Cowdog, the hilarious adventure series about a crime solving ranch dog. Ostensibly for children, the audio renditions by author John R. Erickson are sure to build a cult following among adults as well." — *Parade Magazine*

"Full of regional humor . . . vocals are suitably poignant and ridiculous. A wonderful yarn." — *Booklist*

"For the detectin' and protectin' exploits of the canine Mike Hammer, hang Hank's name right up there with those of other anthropomorphic greats...But there's no sentimentality in Hank: he's just plain more rip-roaring fun than the others. Hank's misadventures as head of ranch security on a spread somewhere in the Texas Panhandle are marvelous situation comedy." — *School Library Journal*

"Knee-slapping funny and gets kids reading."

— *Fort Worth Star Telegram*

The Ranch Life Learning Series

Want to learn more about ranching? Check out Hank's hilarious and educational new series, Ranch Life Learning, brought to you by Maverick Books and The National Ranching Heritage Center!

Saddle up for some fun as the same cast of characters you've come to know and love in the Hank the Cowdog series gives you a first-class introduction to life on a ranch!

In these books, you'll learn things like: the difference between a ranch and a farm, how cows digest grass, what it takes to run a ranch as a successful business, how to take care of cattle throughout the various seasons, what the daily life of a working cowboy looks like, qualities to look for in a good horse, the many kinds of wild animals you might see if you spent a few days on Hank's ranch, the tremendous impact different kinds of weather have on every aspect of ranching, and, last but not least, the consequences and benefits of wildfires!

Love Hank's Hilarious Songs?

Hank the Cowdog's "Greatest Hits" albums bring together the music from the unabridged audiobooks you know and love! These wonderful collections of hilarious (and sometimes touching) songs are unmatched. Where else can you learn about coyote philosophy, buzzard lore, why your dog is protecting an old corncob, how bugs compare to hot dog buns, and much more!

And, be sure to visit Hank's "Music Page" on the official website to listen to some of the songs and download FREE Hank the Cowdog ringtones!

"Audio-Only" Stories

Ever wondered what those "Audio-Only" Stories in Hank's Official Store are all about?

The Audio-Only Stories are Hank the Cowdog adventures that have never been released as books. They are about half the length of a typical Hank book, and there are currently seven of them. They have run as serial stories in newspapers for years and are now available as audiobooks!

Have you visited Hank's official website yet?

www.hankthecowdog.com

Don't miss out on exciting *Hank the Cowdog* games and activities, as well as up-to-date news about upcoming books in the series!

When you visit, you'll find:

- Hank's BLOG, which is the first place we announce upcoming books and new products!
- Hank's Official Shop, with tons of great *Hank the Cowdog* books, audiobooks, games, t-shirts, stuffed animals, mugs, bags, and more!
- Links to Hank's social media, whereby Hank sends out his "Cowdog Wisdom" to fans.
- A FREE, printable "Map of Hank's Ranch"!
- Hank's Music Page where you can listen to songs and even download FREE ringtones!
- A way to sign up for Hank's free email updates
- Sally May's "Ranch Roundup Recipes"!
- Printable & Colorable Greeting Cards for Holidays.

- Articles about Hank and author John R. Erickson in the news,

...AND MUCH, MUCH MORE!

BOOKS
The Collection

FAN ZONE
Fun & Games

AUTHOR
Meet the Creator

STORE
Books & More

Find Toys, Games, Books & More
at the Hank shop.

ANNOUNCING:
A sneak peek at Hank #66

Hank Plays Cupid:

GAMES — COME PLAY WITH HANK & PALS

BOOKS — BROWSE THE ENTIRE HANK CATALOG

FRIENDS — GET TO KNOW THE RANCH GANG

 Visit Hank's Facebook page

 Follow Hank on Twitter

 Watch Hank on YouTube

 Follow Hank on Pinterest

 Send Hank an Email

FROM THE BLOG

JAN 28 Hank is Cupid in Disguise...

JAN 18 The Valentine's Day Robbery! - a Snippet from the Story

DEC 04 Getting SIGNED Hank the Cowdog books for Christmas!

OCT 14 Education Association's lists of recommended books?

Hank's Music.
Free ringtones, music and more!

MORE

VISIT THE BLOG

Hank's Survey
We'd love to know what you think!   GO

Official Shop
Find books, audio, toys and more!

LET'S GO

Get the Latest
Keep up with Hank's news and promotions by signing up for our e-news.
Looking for The Hank Times fan club newsletter?

Enter your email address
SIGN UP

TEACHER'S CORNER
Download fun activity guides, discussion questions and more.

Join Hank's Security Force
Get the activity letter and other cool stuff.

JOIN   SECURITY FORCE

SALLY MAY'S RECIPES
Discover delicious recipes from Sally May herself.   GO

Hank in the News
Find out what the media is saying about Hank.

GO

FEATURED BOOK

The Christmas Turkey Disaster
Now Available!
Hank is in real trouble this time. L...

BUY   READ   LISTEN

BOOKS
Browse Titles
Buy Books
Audio Samples
Other Books

FAN ZONE
Games
Hank & Friends
Security Force
Educational Stuff

AUTHOR
John Erickson's Bio
Hank in the News
In Concert
Contact John

SHOP
The Books
Store
Get Help
Retailer Info

Teacher's Corner

Know a teacher who uses Hank in their classroom? You'll want to be sure they know about Hank's "Teacher's Corner"! Just click on the link on the homepage, and you'll find free teacher's aids, such as a printable map of Hank's ranch, a reading log, coloring pages, blog posts specifically for teachers and librarians, quizzes and much more!

The Very Best Toy

by Gary Rinker
A Picture Book for Young Readers

What is the very best toy? Playing with Dad! Through a child's imagination, a dad becomes a swing, a horse, a slide, a trampoline and more!

Get your copy today in Hank's Store:
www.hankthecowdog.com

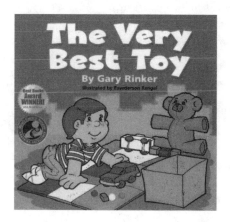

Mom's Choice Award Winner!

Best Books 2011 Award Winner in Children's Picture Book from USA News

Join Hank the Cowdog's Security Force

Are you a big Hank the Cowdog fan? Then you'll want to join Hank's Security Force. Here is some of the neat stuff you will receive:

Welcome Package
- A Hank paperback of your choice
- An original Hank poster (19" x 25")
- A Hank bookmark

Eight digital issues of *The Hank Times* newspaper with
- Lots of great games and puzzles
- Stories about Hank and his friends
- Special previews of future books
- Fun contests

More Security Force Benefits
- Special discounts on Hank books, audios, and more
- Special Members Only section on Hank's website at www.hankthecowdog.com

Total value of the Welcome Package and *The Hank Times* is $23.99. However, your two-year membership is **only $7.99** plus $5.00 for shipping and handling.

☐ Yes, I want to join Hank's Security Force. Enclosed is $12.99 ($7.99 + $5.00 for shipping and handling) for my **two-year membership**. [Make check payable to Maverick Books. International shipping extra.]

WHICH BOOK WOULD YOU LIKE TO RECEIVE IN YOUR WELCOME PACKAGE? CHOOSE ANY BOOK IN THE SERIES. (EXCEPT #50)   (#   )

_____   BOY or GIRL
YOUR NAME   (CIRCLE ONE)

_____
MAILING ADDRESS

_____
CITY   STATE   ZIP

_____
TELEPHONE   BIRTH DATE

_____
E-MAIL   (REQUIRED FOR DIGITAL HANK TIMES)

Send check or money order for $12.99 to:

Hank's Security Force
Maverick Books
P.O. Box 549
Perryton, Texas 79070
Offer is subject to change

DO NOT SEND CASH.   NO CREDIT CARDS ACCEPTED.
ALLOW 2-3 WEEKS FOR DELIVERY

The following activities are samples from *The Hank Times*, the official newspaper of Hank's Security Force. Please do not write on these pages unless this is your book. And, even then, why not just find a scrap of paper?

"Photogenic" Memory Quiz

We all know that Hank has a "photogenic" memory—being aware of your surroundings is an important quality for a Head of Ranch Security. Now *you* can test your powers of observation.

How good is your memory? Look at the illustration on page 8 and try to remember as many things about it as possible. Then turn back to this page and see how many questions you can answer.

1. Open or Closed mouth for: Hank? Drover? Slim?

2. Was Slim wearing a cowboy hat?

3. Which was bigger? Headlights or Mirrors?

4. Could you see any of the pickup's license plate?

5. Was Hank looking to HIS Left or Right?

6. How many of Slim's hands could you see: 0, 1, 2, or all 4?

"Rhyme Time"

When the rats get chased off the ranch, what kinds of jobs do you think they could find? Make a rhyme using "Rats" that would relate to their new job possibilities.

> *Example: The Rats make large tanks that hold*
> *melted wax for making candles.*
> *Answer: Rats* **VATS.**

1. The Rats start a baseball supply company.

2. The Rats open a tire repair shop.

3. The Rats host a weekend getaway retreat spot.

4. The Rats' track team's shooting percentages and lots of other numbers.

5. The Rats provide a feline adoption business.

6. The Rats teach kids the best way to pet their dogs.

7. The Rats open a counseling service to help settle arguments.

8. The Rats make things to put by your front door that say Welcome.

Answers:

1. Rats BATS
2. Rats PLATS
3. Rats SATS
4. Rats STATS
5. Rats CATS
6. Rats PATS
7. Rats SPATS
8. Rats MATS

"Photogenic" Memory Quiz

We all know that Hank has a "photogenic" memory—being aware of your surroundings is an important quality for a Head of Ranch Security. Now *you* can test your powers of observation.

How good is your memory? Look at the illustration on the cover of this book and try to remember as many things about it as possible. Then turn back to this page and see how many questions you can answer.

1. Was Hank looking Up, Down or Straight Ahead?

2. Were there any clouds in the sky?

3. How many cows could you see? 1, 2, 3, or 4?

4. Which of Slim's hands was higher? HIS Left or Right?

5. Could you see any pockets on Slim's coat?

6. How many of Hank's feet could you see? 0, 1, 2, 4 or 5?

"Word Maker"

Try making up to twenty words from the letters in the names below. Use as many letters as possible, however, don't just add an "s" to a word you've already listed in order to have it count as another. Try to make up entirely new words for each line!

Then, count the total number of letters used in all of the words you made, and see how well you did using the Security Force Rankings below!

PETE   RATS

_____	_____
_____	_____
_____	_____
_____	_____
_____	_____
_____	_____
_____	_____
_____	_____
_____	_____
_____	_____

55 - 61 You spend too much time with J.T. Cluck and the chickens.

62 - 65 You are showing some real Security Force potential.

66 - 69 You have earned a spot on our Ranch Security team.

70 +   Wow! You rank up there as a top-of-the-line cowdog.

John R. Erickson,

Photo Courtesy of Western Horseman Magazine

a former cowboy, has written numerous books for both children and adults and is best known for his acclaimed *Hank the Cowdog* series. The *Hank* series began as a self-publishing venture in Erickson's garage in 1982 and has endured to become one of the nation's most popular series for children and families.

Through the eyes of Hank the Cowdog, a smelly, smart-aleck Head of Ranch Security, Erickson gives readers a glimpse into daily life on a cattle ranch in the West Texas Panhandle. His stories have won a number of awards, including the Audie, Oppenheimer, Wrangler, and Lamplighter Awards, and have been translated into Spanish, Danish, Farsi, and Chinese. In 2019, Erickson was inducted into the Texas Literary Hall of Fame. *USA Today* calls the *Hank the Cowdog* books "the best family entertainment in years." Erickson lives and works on his ranch in Perryton, Texas, with his family.

Nicolette G. Earley

Photo by Kris Erickson

was born and raised in the Texas Hill Country. She began working for Maverick Books in 2008, editing, designing new Hank the Cowdog books, and working with the artist who had put faces on all the characters: Gerald Holmes. When Holmes died in 2019, she discovered that she could reproduce his drawing style and auditioned for the job. She made her debut appearance in Book 75, illustrating new books in the series she read as a child. She and her husband, Keith, now live in coastal Mississippi.